THE LEFT-HANDED SHELL

When Harry, a small-time detective, agrees to look after Jenny and her friend Jacintha — the daughter of a millionaire — little does he realise that he and his giant-sized cousin Stanley are going to become involved in a kidnapping. The girls must be found, and what at first seems to be a straightforward kidnapping becomes more complicated. Why are all these people being killed? Where are the girls? Who are the kidnappers, and what has a left-handed shell to do with all this?

JAMES GRANT

THE LEFT-HANDED SHELL

Complete and Unabridged

LINFORD
Leicester

First published in Great Britain

First Linford Edition
published 2001

British Library CIP Data

Grant, James, *1933* –
    The left-handed shell.—Large print ed.—
Linford mystery library
1. Detective and mystery stories
2. Large type books
I. Title
823.9'14 [F]

ISBN 0–7089–4555–4

Published by
F. A. Thorpe (Publishing)
Anstey, Leicestershire

Set by Words & Graphics Ltd.
Anstey, Leicestershire
Printed and bound in Great Britain by
T. J. International Ltd., Padstow, Cornwall

This book is printed on acid-free paper

1

Apart from the seagulls there were not many signs of life on the beach.

To the north of where I stood, the shore line curved gently outwards towards the promentory that marked the southern end of the next bay. It was about two and a half miles to the point and there was no human life in sight.

Away to my right, the south, the beach stretched straight until it disappeared in the faintly grey haze of a late November afternoon. There were two figures walking along the shore, close to the water's edge. They hadn't been there a few minutes before so I knew they were coming towards me, but they were still too far away for me to know what sex they were.

I was standing beside a large block of concrete that had once formed part of an old wartime machine-gun emplacement in the faint hope that it would give me some shelter from the wind. It didn't. The wind, driving in off the North Sea, was cold and strong and wasn't going to be put off by a little thing like that. I shivered and stamped my feet on the wet sand and tried to look as if I was enjoying myself.

There wasn't any doubt that my three companions were enjoying themselves. In fact they appeared to be having the time of their lives, but then I suppose a force eight gale has less effect on the games of twelve-year olds than it does on someone three and half times that age.

One of the twelve-year olds was the reason for my being there in the first place. Jenny Andrews is the daughter of Tommy Andrews, and Tommy is one of the few friends I have. Tommy is a civil engineer and, as his job takes him to all parts of the country, his home life had been erratic for more years than he could remember. A few years earlier his wife had been killed in a car crash and Tommy, at a loss to know how to cope with his young daughter, had solved the twin problems of education and accommodation by putting her into a residential private school on the outskirts of a village near Scarborough. He lived a simple life and had few expenses and, as the firm he worked for thought highly of him and paid him a lot of money, he could afford it.

His contacts with Jenny were regular; every two weeks he would drive up to North Yorkshire, take her out of school on a Friday afternoon and spend the weekend with her, returning her to the safe-keeping of the school by tea-time Sunday. He never missed.

At least he didn't until he fell into a foundation trench at the power-station site he was running, and fractured both legs. That was where I came in. He asked me to deputise for him on his fortnightly ritual visits. It hadn't appealed to me because I'm unaccustomed to the company of children and I seldom know what to say, or do, to keep them amused. Fortunately Jenny was very self-possessed and mature for her years and as Tommy was a good friend and as he also employed my cousin Stanley when most people wouldn't, I had agreed.

This was the fifth weekend I'd stood in

for Tommy and I was relieved that it was also the last. Tommy's casts were due to come off in a few days and, with luck, he would be walking, or at least driving his car, before the next two weeks had passed. My child-minding days were almost over.

The second twelve-year-old was one of Jenny's school friends. Her name was Jacintha Gannon, fortunately everyone called her Jackie. Her father was Carl Gannon. I'd heard of him. Who hadn't? He was an American, but resident, most of the time, in this country. He was the only son of Reinhardt Gannon who had died a few years earlier at the age of ninety after having turned the small fortune his father had left him into several billions of dollars. The old man had been the tenth richest man in the world and as he had left everything to his son that now made Carl Gannon the tenth richest man in the world. Also, if what the Sunday supplements said was right, he was already climbing up the table. In a position where ambition seemed a pointless characteristic, he seemed to have a lot of it.

The third and last human playing on the cold, windswept beach was my cousin Stanley. He seemed to be enjoying it more than the others, but then he hadn't had very many opportunities to play games, certainly not when we were kids, and never since then either.

The fourth player in the game was a small, extremely agressive and bad-tempered Scottish Terrier named Mister Mackay. He belonged to Jenny Andrews and spent his weekdays with Tommy, angrily snapping at the ankles of anyone who dared enter his site office without taking the precaution of wearing Wellingtons. The dog was an unfortunately obligatory accompaniment to the task of collecting Jenny for the weekend. On the few occasions I had stood in for Tommy it had managed to nip me on three of them and there existed between us a state of undeclared war.

I looked at Stanley as the game they were playing reached a crescendo of shouts and laughter. Somehow, to me at least, he didn't seem out of place playing there with the two little girls and the small dog, even though his massive bulk towered over them. Stanley is one of the biggest men I have ever seen. Well over six and a half feet tall, he was built like the concrete block I stood against, solid and seemingly impregnable.

The game ended and they came across the sand towards me. The two girls were flushed, still apparently impervious to the wind. I looked at them. Jenny, fair-haired and blue-eyed, was very bright. Her mind was sharp and, surprisingly for me, some of the time I felt more at ease with her than with many adults. She had a maturity well beyond her years. Her friend Jackie, black-haired and dark-eyed, was also quite bright, but she hadn't the same assurance that Tommy's daughter had. That struck me as odd. I would have thought that the daughter of one of the world's richest men would have oozed with confidence, even at her age.

Stanley came last. He seemed reluctant to stop playing the game. He was the same age as me and in any gathering his size and the immense strength that accompanied it were impressive. The trouble with him was, that of the three, he was probably the closest to being a real twelve-year-old. Although his body had grown enormously his mind had stopped developing when we were still kids at school, and it had never picked up again. That was why he was with me, why he was always with me. Someone had to look after him and that someone was me; partly because there was no one else and partly because I didn't have a lot of choice, morally speaking that is.

Jenny reached me first. 'What time is it Uncle Harry?' she asked.

I looked at my watch. 'Four o'clock. Time we were off.'

'Must we?'

'We'd better, you know what Simpson's like.' The expressions on the faces of the two girls said, Yes they did know what Simpson was like.

Jackie Gannon came out of school at the same times as Jenny, but her father never came to collect her. I gathered that sometimes her mother came, but every time I'd been there Gannon's chauffeur had turned up alone in one of the fleet of expensive motor cars maintained by Gannon's company, International Oil. The chauffeur's name was Ronald Simpson, tall and quite good-looking, he was something of an old woman — a born worrier. During the previous couple of visits I'd got into casual conversation with him and when I had found that on this particular Friday he wouldn't be able to reach the school until three hours after the girls had got out, I had suggested that Jackie could come with us. We always started with a visit to the beach to enable Jenny to look for shells for her collection. I had told Simpson to come to the car park above the beach and we would meet him there at four o'clock. He had chewed over it for a few minutes and then, when the girls had ganged up on him, he had agreed, but only so long as we didn't tell his boss. As my chances of ever meeting Carl Gannon had seemed extremely remote it had been an easy promise to make.

We walked south along the beach towards the steps that led up to the clifftop and I noticed the couple I had seen earlier had almost reached us. I could see they were a man and a woman, both in their middle fifties. They looked at us with the mixture of diffidence and embarrassment the British usually managed to produce for meetings when it is almost impossible to completely ignore their fellow human beings. They looked at Stanley with some interest and surprise and when the woman's eyes caught mine she smiled nervously. They went up the steps ahead of us and so that we didn't crowd them on the way up I gave in to Jenny's request for a few more minutes shell-hunting along the beach.

She went off, with Stanley a highly delighted and co-operative companion. The other girl didn't seem very keen, but went along for their company. After all, the only alternative was to stay and talk to me and that would've been a very one-sided conversation.

The interest in shell-collecting shared by Jenny and Stanley, was a relatively recent development, at least it was as far as Stanley was concerned. Jenny had started a few years before and I remembered hearing her talk about it to her father. Stanley was, however, a collector of many years standing, but not of shells. He collected junk, although even that title was a bit grandiose for the rubbish he brought home. We had lived in a rented cottage in Surrey where there were several outbuildings which he had gradually filled up with anything that caught his eye. I had tried to talk him out of it on several occasions, but had failed, maybe because I hadn't tried all that hard. After all it was a harmless enough hobby and I couldn't grudge him that small concession towards acceptance of his state of mind.

Unfortunately we had moved from the cottage with its accommodating out-houses and until I found us a reasonable place to live, close to the site where Stanley was now working, we were using an elderly caravan that had provided shelter for us during similar problem times in the past. Stanley's collecting bug was still in full spate and as we no longer had anywhere for him to keep the things

10

he usually brought home — the old bicycle frames, bits of motor cars, packing cases, oven doors and the like — he had begun to get a bit morose. Casting around for a new hobby for him I had remembered Jenny's shell-collecting and that had turned out to be just the thing he needed. In many ways it was more than just a substitute for his rubbish-gathering, it was a step forward.

Although he had spent almost as many years at school as Tommy and I, very little had sunk in after the first few years simply because he had reached the limits of his restricted intellect. Once or twice in later years I had tried to improve things by sending him along to special classes for adults but there didn't seem to be anything that was geared to his particular kind of problem. He wasn't simple-minded and he wasn't stupid. He was alert and good with his hands, particularly as far as the internal combustion-engine was concerned, an area where he made me look like an aborigine. I suppose I should have accepted that he was what he was, and I have to admit most of the time I did just that, but occasionally I had a sudden burst of conscience and tried to do something more for him than I usually did.

Like most bursts of consciousness it was somewhat misplaced as he was happier when I did nothing than when I was thrusting him into places he didn't want to go, like school.

I watched the three of them walking along the tide-line and reflected that a stranger watching them would have a very different view to the one I had. The stranger would see a man whose physical appearance was such that he would impress to the point of frightening almost anyone he met. In fact Stanley would run from trouble far more readily than either of the two girls were likely to. At least he did so most of the time. Occasionally, and fortunately it was on very infrequent occasions, he wouldn't run from trouble. That was when life became difficult for both of us.

I glanced up the steps towards the clifftop. The couple had disappeared from sight and I called out to the girls and

Stanley and reluctantly they came back towards me.

'Time we were off,' I said.

'Must we, Uncle Harry?'

'Afraid so.'

There were three almost identical expressions of mingled annoyance and acceptance that the world of grown-ups was intruding once again into real life, but then they turned towards the foot of the steps and I followed. Unfortunately, however, Mister Mackay chose that very moment to hurtle off along the beach in hot pursuit of a herring gull that was very nearly as big as he was.

'I'll get him Harry,' Stanley shouted and ran off after the dog.

'We're going back to the car park,' I yelled after his retreating figure. If he answered, it was lost in the sound of the wind. I turned and trudged back across the sand towards the steps and with the two girls ahead of me, climbed slowly to the top. Or rather I climbed slowly, they ran most of the way.

There were only two cars in the car park. My Volvo estate and a Rolls Royce

Silver Cloud. The driver's door opened as we approached and Simpson came hurrying towards us, his face lined with worry that made him look a lot older than his real age that I'd estimated at about thirty-five.

'You're late,' he snapped peevishly at me.

'You worry too much.'

'Four o'clock is four o'clock, not half past.'

I shrugged my shoulders without bothering to reply. The two girls had opened the rear door of the Rolls and were busily opening up the cocktail cabinet and exploring its contents. Simpson walked round and climbed into the driver's seat and started the engine. I stuck my head inside the rear compartment and took Jenny's hand.

'Can't we wait until Stanley brings Mister Mackay?' she asked me.

'Yes, we have to wait until then Simpson,' Jackie put in.

The chauffeur's head jerked round. 'Who the hell is Mister Mackay?' he asked.

I looked at him and said, 'Mister Mackay is a dog. To be precise he's a Scottish Terrier.' He looked vaguely relieved and turned off the ignition. It began to drizzle and I climbed into the back of the Silver Cloud and pulled the door shut.

The girls were chattering excitedly about the current Top Twenty and most of their conversation didn't mean a lot to me. I gathered that one of Jackie's favourite singers, Simon Black, was appearing locally that weekend and she was a bit miffed that for one reason or another she wouldn't be able to see him.

It was about ten minutes before Stanley appeared and by then Simpson had begun to fidget and look at his watch. I opened the door and went to meet Stanley. There was no sign of the little black dog.

'I'm sorry Harry, I couldn't catch him and he wouldn't come when I called.' He looked abject about his failure.

I grinned at him. 'Don't worry about it. I'll get him. You get in the car out of the rain.' I went out of the car park and back to the top of the steps that led down to the beach. I could see the dog, a small black shape, about half a mile away, hurtling in and out of the water, sending up clouds of presumably irate seagulls at every dash. I went down the steps, carefully, as they were becoming slippery with the drizzle that was being compounded by the spray the wind was whipping off the waves.

By the time I got within shouting distance of the dog I was wet and irritable. The dog took no notice of me and after several abortive attempts to grab him as he dashed in and out of the water my irritability had shifted a few notches into anger. After a while the dog decided that avoiding me was a better game than chasing seagulls and he devoted his full attention to the matter. For his part the game consisted of running full tilt for my feet and then turning off at the last second and sprinting off at right angles with his tail held protectively low in case one of my feet should make contact with his backside.

Finally, one despairing lunge carried

me beyond the point of balance and I fell on my knees into a pool of water. That proved to be the breaking point and I screamed something at the dog that must have contained the right proportions of rage and command because he came trotting up to me and tentatively licked one of my hands. I risked total immersion, grabbed at him and pulled him in under my arm, scrambled to my feet and headed back to the cliff steps.

By the time I reached the top for the second time that afternoon I was soaking wet, covered in sand and decidedly out of breath. If it hadn't been the last of my visits to entertain Jenny, I would have made it the last. All my pre-conceptions about dogs and children were being upheld.

I had my head down, my collar pulled high to keep out some of the rain, and I was inside the car park before I looked up.

The Rolls Royce Silver Cloud had gone.

For a brief moment of time I assumed that Simpson had tired of waiting and had gone off with Jackie, leaving Jenny and Stanley to wait for me, but there was nobody inside the Volvo and there were no other cars in sight. I stood there for several seconds, my mind considering and rejecting all the acceptable possibilities. I was just getting round to considering the unacceptable when I saw a movement behind my car. I started across the flat, glistening, tarmacadamed surface, and as I did so I saw that the movement had been made by a man, half hidden by the car. I ran forward and as I rounded the Volvo, I saw that it was Stanley.

He was sitting on the ground, his long legs stretched out in front of him, one huge hand trying to take a grip on the wing of the car so that he could pull himself to his feet. Blood was streaming down his face from a wound across his forehead.

I dropped to my knees beside him and then realised I still had the dog under my arm. I fumbled in my pocket for my keys, unlocked the door and heaved the animal inside. Then I turned back to Stanley. His eyes were closed and I reached out and touched him. Instantly one of his hands siezed mine and gripped.

'Stanley, it's me. Harry.' After a moment his grip relaxed and after another pause his eyes opened and I could sense the effort it took.

He focussed on me. 'Harry, I'm sorry, I tried . . . '

'Tell me what happened,' I cut in.

'Two men . . . hit me . . . Jenny screamed . . . I heard them drive away.'

'Okay, Stanley. Don't say anything else for a moment.' I stood up and felt for the car keys and then realised they were still in the car door. I took them out and went round and unlocked the tailgate. Then I went back to Stanley and somehow I managed to half-drag him to the back of the car. Fortunately he kept getting back little bursts of consciousness and eventually I had him sitting on the deck and from there he crawled far enough into the car for me to close the door. I clambered into the driving seat, pulled the seat forward because Stanley had driven from the school, and started the engine.

I glanced over my shoulder. Stanley

was lying on his back, his eyes closed. Mister Mackay, the Scottie, had scrambled over the back of the seat and was lying beside Stanley, carefully licking his hand. Even though it was the dog's fault that I hadn't been there when it had happened, I felt some sort of affection for it at that moment.

As I swung the car out of the car park my brain was trying to function on several different levels at the same time. I knew Stanley needed medical attention. I knew Tommy had to be told and I knew Jackie's father, Carl Gannon, had to be told. I also knew the police should be told and that was the part of my thinking that was causing most trouble at that moment.

I didn't need anyone to tell me that I was mixed up in a kidnapping which was the kind of thing best handled by the police. But I also knew enough to know that right at the top of the list of demands made by kidnappers was, don't tell the police. But it was a demand that was made of the family of the victim. That meant it wasn't my decision, but it was still one I had to face.

2

As it turned out I didn't have to make the decision after all. I was on the road leading towards the main coast road when I worked out that my best course of action was to go back to the school. It was nearer than the nearest hospital and I knew that they had permanent medical staff there; also I would be able to telephone from there and, while there were one or two farms and isolated houses closer to hand, I didn't want to involve any complete outsiders at this stage of the proceedings. I made it to the school in ten minutes and within another half minute I was inside the Principal's office giving orders. Fortunately the Principal was a fierce woman with the face and build of a regimental sergeant-major and who, at a glance, took in the fact that I wasn't banging around for the fun of it.

She got onto one of the two telephones

on her desk and snapped out orders that soon had a rather fluttery, but apparently competent, nurse bathing Stanley's face while two male porters made him as comfortable as possible where he lay in the back of the car. We went back into her office.

'I'll call the police now,' I said.

'What happened to Jenny?' I hesitated, but she went on, 'You'd better tell me. After all my responsibility doesn't end the moment they walk out through that door.'

She didn't look the type to fall apart when things got rough, so I told her what had happened. Or to be precise I told her what I knew and what I had assumed had happened while I was chasing the dog on the beach.

'I think it will be best if you speak to the parents first,' she said. 'After that, depending on what is said, we can contact the police. I know we're supposed to help the police, but in my view the parents should have the choice.'

I shook my head slowly. 'The police will need all the help they can get on a case like this, and a flying start is about the only help I can give them.'

'Call the parents,' she said firmly. 'Five minutes won't make a lot of difference.' I wasn't too sure that I agreed with her, but part of me wanted to avoid doing anything that might endanger the lives of the two girls. At that moment, from the point of safety, there didn't seem to be very much choice between the two courses of action open to me.

I called Tommy first because I had his number in my diary and I outlined what had happened, playing down the attack on Stanley. Tommy didn't miss the point of that, however.

'If they laid Stanley out then they're not playing games Harry,' he said after a long silence, during which he assimilated my news. He paused again and I waited, listening to the static humming on the line. 'I'll be there as soon as I can,' he went on, a slight shake in his voice. 'It will take me about two hours in the car, but add an hour because I'll have to get someone to take me to the hospital first and get these casts off.'

'Tommy . . . ' I broke off, uncertain what to say.

'Not your fault Harry,' he said. 'You didn't know anything like this would happen. Anyway, it's pretty obvious they wanted the other girl, Jenny's friend. Have you talked to her father?'

'Not yet.' I paused. 'I haven't talked to the police yet either.'

'It's difficult,' he said, and I knew that he was torn between the two courses of action in the way I had been. 'Talk to Gannon,' he went on. 'I'll go along with him at this stage.'

'I'll see you later then.'

'Yes. I'll be there in about three hours.'

'Watch yourself on the roads,' I said.

His voice was almost inaudible when he answered. 'Don't worry, I'm not going to kill myself, but if the bastards who've done this have harmed her in any way, any way at all, I'll kill them.' He hung up before I could speak again.

I depressed the rest and looked at the card the school's Principal had taken from a file cabinet and then dialled the number on it. After some time a woman answered. She identified herself as Celia Gannon and another quick glance at the card told me that I was talking to Jacintha's mother. She had a warm, pleasant English-accented voice. I told her what had happened. This time I didn't mention Stanley, because she didn't know him and there didn't seem much point in compounding her problems by telling her that violence had already been committed. There would be time for that later when she had people around her to help. Her voice wavered when she spoke after I had finished, but she told me she would contact her husband and he would call me at the school.

I put down the telephone and looked at the stockily built woman at the other side of the desk.

'Gannon will be calling me here,' I said.

'You're not calling the police?'

'Not yet.'

'It will be a difficult choice for the parents.'

'You can say that again.' I stood up. 'I'll go and see how Stanley is getting on. Call me when Gannon rings.'

Outside Stanley was responding to the attention of the nurse. The porters had disappeared. He looked at me as I ducked under the tailgate and scrambled in beside them.

'I'm sorry Harry,' he said quietly.

'That's okay Stanley. None of it was your fault.'

'Will Jenny be all right?'

'Yes of course she will,' I said with a lot more confidence than I felt. The nurse looked at me questioningly. I realised she didn't know what had happened, and there wasn't any point that I could see in getting more people involved than was absolutely necessary. Instead I asked Stanley if he thought he could walk far enough to get inside the building. With some rather ineffectual help from the nurse I got Stanley out of the estate car and upright. Somehow we got him inside, but we didn't have much more control over him than we would have had over a live telegraph pole. One of the porters reappeared and his help was welcome.

None of the school staff had ever seen Stanley out of the car on any of our previous visits and they looked startled at the size of him. Even the Principal allowed a flicker of surprise to cross her face when we entered her office. We sat him in the middle of an expensive-looking leather settee that stood against one wall of her office.

'Do you think brandy will help?' she asked.

'No thank you. He doesn't drink and I don't want to risk giving him something he isn't used to.' She raised an enquiring eyebrow, but I didn't feel inclined to spend time telling her about Stanley's problems. I went back out to the car and found Mister Mackay had jumped down from the open rear door and was wandering around sniffing the tyres. I waited until he had found the one best suited to his purpose and then put him back inside and closed the doors. He decided that he'd had enough of the car for the time being and started barking furiously. I ignored him and went back into the building.

As I opened the door to the Principal's office the telephone began to ring. She answered it and it was obviously Gannon and equally obviously he was giving her a hard time. I reached out and took the instrument from her. Gannon's voice was harsh, his accent that of an American who had spent a lot of time somewhere other than the United States. I cut in and told him who I was and what had happened. I didn't miss out the part about Stanley being attacked. When I'd finished there was a moment of silence.

When he spoke his voice was still harsh, but not so loud. 'Have you told the police?'

'Not yet.'

'Then don't.' It was a command from a man who sounded as if he gave a lot of them and was seldom, if ever, disobeyed.

'When will you get here?' I asked instead of quibbling over his manner.

'I'm in a meeting now. It should be over in half an hour. I'll fly up. I'll be there later this evening.'

'Okay,' I said.

'Remember Morgan, I said no police.'

'You're not the only one involved,' I said mildly.

'What? You mean the other girl's father. Does he know?'

'Yes.'

'Does he want the police?'

'Not yet.'

'Good, we'll keep it that way.' He replaced the telephone before I had a chance to say anything else. It was probably as well. I don't often take an instant dislike to people, least of all on the strength of nothing more than a telephone conversation, but I knew that I was going to make an exception in the case of Carl Gannon.

Something of my thoughts must have shown in my face because the school Principal nodded at the telephone before saying, 'A difficult man.'

'Yes.' I tried a smile, but it didn't work very well. 'I'm sorry,' I went on. 'I don't know your name.'

'Mrs Jennings.'

'He'll be here later, so will Jenny's father. Until then there isn't very much we can do.' I glanced at Stanley who was beginning to look a little healthier. 'I think I'll spend some of the time finding out what Stanley remembers.' I hesitated.

'Would you like me to leave?' she asked. That was exactly what I did want, but it hadn't seemed very polite to ask.

'Perhaps there is somewhere we can go?' I asked.

'No, stay here. There are telephones and that settee is about the only seat in the building that will be strong enough to support him.' She headed for the door.

'The fewer people who know about this the better,' I said.

She turned round. 'Don't worry,' she said, 'I will tell the nurse and the porters that you had a slight road accident after you had dropped Jenny off at your home and that she is being taken care of by your wife.'

I nodded my head and she closed the door. The story would serve and the fact that my home was a caravan parked in a farmer's field a few miles outside York and that, whatever else I had picked up over the years, I didn't have a wife, wasn't known to any of the people here.

I went over and sat on the settee beside Stanley. He tried a smile and it came off a little better than mine had a few minutes before.

'How are you feeling?'

'My head aches, Harry.' I nodded and looked closely at the injury. There was a long mark across his forehead that was already swelling and discolouring. The skin had split along part of the swelling and, although the nurse had mopped the blood from his face, there were still droplets oozing from the wound, but they seemed to be congealing.

'Tell me what happened?'

He scowled with concentration. The effort caused his forehead to crease and that must have hurt him because he stopped, but not before the blood began to trickle down his face again. I mopped at it with my handkerchief.

'I went to the car like you told me,' he said. 'I remember we were all going to have a drink of lemonade from the cabinet. Then . . . ' He broke off.

'Yes,' I said gently.

'Jenny screamed,' he said miserably.

'Then what?'

'Someone hit me.'

'Think carefully Stanley. What made Jenny scream?'

'Because someone hit me,' he said.

'In that case she couldn't have screamed first,' I said. He looked hurt and confused. 'Okay Stanley,' I went on. 'Don't get upset about it. Just start at the beginning and tell me everything that you can remember.'

Slowly and hesitantly he did as I had asked and after about ten minutes I had a fairly clear idea of what had happened, but the information didn't seem to give me anything that would be of value. I broke off when there was a rap at the door and Mrs. Jennings strode in accompanied by the nurse.

'I think we'd better have a dressing on your friend's injury,' Mrs. Jennings said. I left the nurse to get on with it and, while she was smearing some ointment on the wound and unrolling a bandage around Stanley's head, one of the porters who had helped earlier came in with a tea tray. I felt the need of something stronger by then and the Principal must have read my mind because as soon as the porter was out of the room she produced a bottle of scotch and poured out a generous measure for me. Then, after the nurse had left, she poured a smaller one for herself.

'Where have they taken Jenny?' Stanley asked suddenly.

'I don't know,' I told him.

'They won't hurt her will they?'

'No, they won't hurt her.'

'If they do I'll hurt them,' the words came out with all the force of a small boy, angry with another child, and I glanced at the Principal. She looked from me to Stanley and back again. Her expression showed a professional interest.

'I'll tell you later,' I said softly to her before turning back to Stanley. 'Don't worry Stanley. Tommy will soon be here and we can start to look for Jenny then.' I hadn't picked a very good moment to mention Tommy. Stanley's face clouded.

'Will Tommy be angry with me?'

'No,' I said and meant it. Tommy would be angry, but it would be a controlled anger and it would be directed towards the right quarter, not at Stanley, who as far as I was able to gather had simply got in the way of a carefully planned kidnapping.

Mrs Jennings poured out tea for all of us and we sat there, each with our own thoughts. Mine were not very progressive. I didn't know what to do. Even though I earned my living as a private enquiry agent, my line of business was very much the low end of the detection scale-kidnappings didn't come into my world. I knew only two things about them. One was that the police should be told and the other was that until the kidnappers made their demands there wasn't a lot to be done. I hadn't done the former and it didn't seem likely that I would be involved in the latter, when they made them. It was obvious too that the demands would be made of Gannon and he hadn't sounded like the kind of man who would want me hanging around when the action started.

Then I remembered what he had said on the telephone. I wondered what kind of man it was that could go back to finish a meeting when he had just been told that his daughter had been kidnapped.

It seemed to me that he wouldn't have much regard for others involved in the case and, as the most important other person involved was Tommy's daughter, who had been in my care, I would have to give Tommy all the support and help he wanted; whether Gannon liked it or not.

3

I was alone in the Principal's office when Tommy arrived. Mrs. Jennings had persuaded me that Stanley should be examined by someone a little higher up the medical ladder than the school's resident nurse. She had called the doctor retained by the school and who lived half a mile down the road towards the centre of the village. He came along, examined Stanley and made noises about X-Rays. He merely nodded when I told him about Stanley and Mrs. Jennings looked interested. The doctor was a little concerned about the fact that Stanley seemed to be worked up about something. I didn't volunteer any information and neither did Mrs. Jennings. The doctor settled for advising me to ensure that Stanley rested and didn't get too excited about anything for a day or two.

After he had gone Mrs. Jennings insisted on making arrangements for

Stanley to lie down. He was too big for a normal-sized bed and when I told her that I overcame that problem at home by putting mattresses on the floor, she took him along to the school's gymnasium, where she planned to make him lie down on one of the big mattresses the pupils used to break their falls when they were using the various pieces of apparatus they had in there.

She was gone a long time and I was glad of the opportunity to try and think of what I could do to help Tommy.

When Tommy came in he looked pale and tense, but he was in control of himself — he usually was. I had known Tommy Andrews for more years than either of us cared to think about. The three of us had gone to school together — him, me and Stanley — and although, over the years, there had been ups and downs in our relationship, we had remained friends, particularly since we had understood and had been able to accept Stanley for what he was.

Tommy was site agent for one of the country's biggest civil engineering contractors and many years before he had offered Stanley a job, and to everyone's surprise it had worked out perfectly for all of us. Stanley was occupied and happy; Tommy had a reliable driver and an expert mechanic for his earth-moving machinery; I had part of the load removed from my mind. I still had to take care of Stanley, but at least there were ten hours a day, five days a week when I could forget all about him.

'Anything happened since we spoke?' Tommy asked me.

'No. I talked to Gannon after I talked to you. He's on his way by now I expect.'

Tommy picked it up at once. 'You expect? You mean there's some doubt about it?'

'No,' I said hastily. 'He's on his way. He said he would fly up. I just don't know when he'll be here.'

'Will the kidnappers know he's here?' Tommy asked, picking up one of the things that I had been thinking about as I waited for him.

'I expect he'll have a pretty comprehensive communications set-up. When they make contact it will be relayed on to him, wherever he is.'

'I suppose so.' Tommy dropped into a chair. 'Jesus. You read about things like this, but you never believe it will happen to you and, even if it did, you're convinced that you'd know how to handle it.' He paused and then looked at me carefully. 'How is Stanley taking it?'

'So far, not too bad. I don't think it has registered fully. He's still a bit shaky from the crack on the head.'

'What happened?'

I told him what I'd been able to reconstruct from the answers Stanley had given to my earlier questioning. 'About ten minutes or so after I'd gone back down to the beach someone yanked open the car door closest to Stanley. He turned round and there were two men. One of the girls screamed, then Stanley was hit and he was aware that he was being pulled out of the car. He started to fight back and then was hit again. Hard. From the mark it left my guess is that it was an iron bar. He went out like a light. When he came to, he was on the ground and the

Rolls had gone. He crawled over to the Volvo and tried to get into it, but he passed out again. Then I came back, I know I was away at least twenty minutes chasing that damned dog so he must have been out, or at least partly out, for ten to fifteen minutes.'

'He didn't see their faces?'

'I don't think so, but I'll talk to him again when he's a bit better. After Gannon gets here.'

'I hope the blow on the head doesn't cause . . . well, I hope he gets over it all right.' I didn't say anything. For a moment we sat there in silence, both thinking about the way Stanley could be on occasions. I knew how much he had enjoyed the weekends we had spent with Jenny. It had surprised me at first, and then pleased me when I realised that he was getting something out of it that he hadn't had before in life, even as a child. I also knew, better even than Tommy, how attached he had become to the little girl. In her own way she had liked him too. She treated him as an equal which wasn't as easy as it sounds. I had a feeling that when he began to recover from the blow on the head and his mind began to grasp the fact that Jenny had been taken away and might be harmed, he might very easily get out of hand. I didn't like to think about what might happen then.

We both heard the cars at the same time and I led the way out into the hallway. There were two vehicles, a car and a Landrover, and seven people, two women and five men.

Gannon was easily identified. He looked exactly like his photographs. Well-built with long arms and a thick neck, he looked more like a wrestler than an oil tycoon. His face was wide, seemingly too wide for his skin which was stretched thinly across prominent cheek-bones. His long fleshless nose and a habit of constantly moving his head from side to side, made him look like a bird of prey on the lookout for its next victim. He had thinning, greyish-blond hair plastered down onto his skull, and pale blue eyes. Even as a baby he wouldn't have won any beauty contests.

'You Morgan?' he asked. I said I was

and he jerked his head and walked into the Principal's office expecting everyone else to follow him. They all did.

One of the women was obviously Celia Gannon, there was a marked resemblence between her and her daughter Jackie. I put her at about thirty-five, maybe fifteen years younger than Gannon. She was fighting to keep control of her emotions and I had the feeling that emotional displays were something that her husband did not tolerate in himself or the people around him, whatever the circumstances. Celia Gannon would have been worth a second look on a happier occasion. She had a wide mouth, large eyes that were darker than blue, but which were not brown. Her skin was very fair and her hair, worn piled high on her head was dark-blonde. Even in those trying circumstances she was extremely attractive, at any other time she would have been a knock-out.

The second woman was young, about twenty-one or two I guessed. She was blonde too, but her version was a yellow colour that looked tawdry beside the older woman. She was pretty in a sulky, spoiled way and I assumed that she was either a companion of Mrs. Gannon's or some kind of secretary.

Three of the men looked like what they probably were — musclemen, there to take orders without questioning them, whatever they might entail. Dressed alike, in plain dark grey suits, white shirts and plain dark ties, they looked alike with hard eyes and mouths in square, expressionless faces.

The fourth man was a very different type. He looked slightly uncomfortable in the well-cut dark blue suit he wore, and it was as if he would have been happier in casual clothes. He had an open-air look about him. His hair was thick and black, his eyes were dark and deep-set and his face was tanned a dark weatherbeaten mahogany.

As he passed me he looked at me carefully, examining, assessing and, I felt, categorising me for future reference. I had the feeling he wasn't all that impressed with what he saw. I looked at Tommy and I could see that Gannon's manner and his

43

two word greeting had affected him in the same way as I had been affected by the telephone conversation with the oil-man earlier. I shrugged my shoulders and went into the office with Tommy close behind me. Mrs. Jennings office was big, but even so it was getting a bit crowded.

Gannon had taken the chair behind the desk and one of the three look-alikes was dialling on the outside line. Mrs Gannon and the girl sat at opposite ends of the settee Stanley had sat in earlier. The remaining look-alikes and the dark complexioned man took up positions around the room. None of them, I noticed, had their backs to windows or the door.

'Tell me again. From the beginning,' Gannon said to me when the man had finished with the telephone and had augmented his companions by taking up a similar, watchful position.

I told him from the beginning. When I came to the part about Stanley being attacked and hurt there was a slight intake of breath from Mrs. Gannon causing her husband's eyes to flick sideways with an expression of irritation crossing his face. When I had finished I introduced Tommy to Gannon. After a slight hesitation Gannon stood up and shook hands with him and then, in case anyone took that as a sign of weakness, he began snapping out orders. The three look-alikes began jumping around like toy dolls making the stillness of the fourth man more noticeable. He had moved forward as I had spoken and was leaning against the corner of the desk, his arms folded across his chest, his deep-set eyes half closed, but, nevertheless, on me all the time.

The three men quickly reorganised the office and brought in from the cars a compact two-way radio transmitter, a tape-recorder and several other pieces of electronic equipment. One of them disappeared for a few minutes and then reappeared with two telephones he seemed to have disconnected from other offices and with the aid of a reel of telephone cable he had brought in from the cars he began to reconnect them on long leads from their original terminals.

Carl Gannon was building himself a communications centre.

In the middle of all this activity Mrs. Jennings came back. She took in the disruption to her office and then looked at Gannon as if to object and then changed her mind. I wasn't sure whether she was afraid to argue, or if she had merely accepted that what was happening was in the best interests of the missing girls.

'The couple on the beach.' The voice was close to my ear, the accent American. I turned my head and the dark-skinned man was standing right behind me. I hadn't heard him come up to me. I started to ask what he was talking about, then I realised he was referring to the middle-aged couple I had mentioned as preceding us up the steps to the cliff-top.

'What about them?'

'Any possible connection?'

'I doubt it.'

'Why do you doubt it?' he asked and I started to get angry and then I realised there was nothing to get angry about, at least not with him. There was no evidence to support my assumption that they were not involved. True, there was nothing to support an assumption that they **were** involved, but I should have known better than to assume the best. If you must assume anything, always assume the worst; that should be one of the mottos of a good detective.

'When I went into the car-park the first time, with the two girls, there were only two cars there. Mine, and Gannon's Rolls. If the couple had a car, and I imagine they had, they had left,' I said.

'Why do you think they had a car?'

'Because that part of the coast is inaccessible other than by one road that leads from the main road to the car park. The road is about two miles long and even when you get to the main road there's nothing there for a pedestrian but an even longer walk. They weren't young so I guess they had a car.'

'If they were already on the beach when you got there then their car must have been in the car park when you first arrived. Was it?'

I looked at my questioner. I had the

unmistakable feeling that whatever it was he did for Gannon, he was a better detective than I was.

'No,' I said quietly. 'There wasn't a car in the car park when we arrived.'

He nodded his head, not triumphantly, just in acceptance that we now had a lead, however tenuous and that was more than we had before he made me start using my brain.

'My name is Parker,' he told me. 'Jay Parker. Where is your friend, Stanley you called him, the one who was attacked?'

'He's my cousin and he's resting.'

'I would like to talk to him. Maybe there is something else he might yet remember.' He managed not to make the remark sound like a criticism.

'I'll go and see how he is. If he's well enough to talk to you I'll bring him back with me.' I told Mrs. Jennings I wanted directions to the gymnasium and she said she would go with me.

The school was mostly in darkness and, as we went through the corridors, she told me that most of the pupils were out for the weekend and those that were not were using just one dormitory to simplify the task of the weekend-duty staff in keeping an eye on them.

In the gymnasium Stanley was looking much better and he seemed eager to help. There was an undercurrent of tension in him that was probably unnoticeable to anyone but me. I hoped that it wasn't the first sign of something worse. He was too big and too strong to control if he got out of hand.

I led the way back towards the office.

'Mr Gannon is not an easy man to deal with,' Mrs. Jennings said, rephrasing her earlier comment.

'No, but then the circumstances are not very good are they?'

'Whatever the circumstances,' she said quietly, more to herself than to me. 'Mrs Gannon is a nice woman, but she doesn't . . . he keeps her . . . ' she broke off, aware that she was committing the unpardonable sin of gossiping.

'Who are the others?' I asked to save her embarrassment.

'I've never seen any of them. Apart from the other daughter, of course.'

I looked at her in surprise. 'Other daughter?'

'Yes. The young woman is Lucinda Gannon, Mr Gannon's daughter by his first marriage. Celia Gannon is his second wife. Jacintha is their daughter.'

'Oh,' I said. It didn't seem important.

When we reached the office there was more tension in the air than there had been when we left and, for a moment, I thought there must have been some contact from the kidnappers. Then I realised from their positions and expressions that Gannon and Tommy had been arguing. I waited in case they wanted to continue and when they didn't I turned round to introduce Stanley to everyone.

He must have made an impressive sight as he ducked his head to walk in through the doorway. There was a trace of blood showing through the bandage and he looked a bit unsteady, but he tried his best to smile at everyone.

I looked around the room. Over the years I had found that the way people reacted to Stanley was a good guide to the kind of person they were. The first reaction, to his size, was almost always the same, but there were a few variations. They were present then. Gannon and his wife showed straight-forward surprise. The three musclemen moved, almost imperceptibly, into better positions in case they had to protect their boss. The other woman, the one I now knew to be Lucinda Gannon, changed her position on the settee, recrossed her legs and then the tip of her tongue came into sight as she let it flicker along her lower lip — that wasn't uncommon either. Jay Parker's expression didn't alter. I had a feeling it never would.

The second reaction they would have to Stanley would come later, when they all realised that, mentally, he wasn't a match for his physical appearance.

Gannon was the first to speak. 'Okay, what happened?' he demanded, his beaky nose jutting forward at Stanley.

'I'll ask the questions,' I said quietly.

'The hell you will,' Gannon snapped at me without turning his head.

'And the hell with you Mr. Gannon,' I said as politely as I could manage. 'I said

I will ask Stanley the questions and that's precisely what I meant.' That brought his head round to me. His expression showed surprise, but I don't think it was surprise that it was me that had argued so much as surprise that anyone at all had done so.

'What's the matter, the big guy hasn't got a tongue of his own?' His voice seemed to be coarsening with every word, all traces of his thin veneer of civility dropping away.

'Just leave it to me,' I said and turned back to Stanley. Gannon wasn't prepared to leave it to anybody, least of all me. He stormed around the desk and marched up to Stanley and jabbed his finger into his chest. The top of his head came level with Stanley's shoulders and he wasn't a small man. The three dark-suited men eased forward, ready to move in when it became necessary. It didn't because Stanley backed away, an expression that combined bewilderment and fear coming onto his face. He looked anxiously at me.

'Harry, can't we go now and look for Jenny?' The words, and more obviously, the tone they were spoken in told everyone the truth about Stanley and I got the second reaction I had been waiting for.

The three musclemen relaxed visibly, they knew they wouldn't have any trouble from that quarter.

Again, Parker's expression didn't alter.

Lucinda Gannon looked disappointed, as if she was a child who had been shown a new toy and then learned that it wasn't for her.

Her step-mother's expression showed compassion. That was less common.

Stanley and I had been together for a long, long time. From the day his mother died in fact, and as that was the day he was born I'm talking about a lifetime. Not that I knew very much about the early days, after all, I was only three weeks old myself at the time.

It was during our schooldays that Stanley became more noticeably different to all the other kids. Until then it hadn't been very obvious, even to me. Maybe I wasn't very bright myself at the time, but I think that it was more likely that my parents, who had taken Stanley in from the start, treated him in such a way that it was never apparent that he was what some people like to call mentally retarded.

Once I did realise what he was like, things got a bit rough . . . for him. Well, you know what small boys are like, thoughtless and mindless when it comes to other people's problems. I was like all the rest, tormenting and aggravating him, but he never seemed to mind. He just smiled and tried to be friendly with everyone. Then one day when I was being attacked by a gang in the school yard, he came to my rescue and very nearly killed one of them. That one was Tommy Andrews. If it seems odd that Tommy held Stanley in high regard, now that we were all a lot older, it is simply evidence that human nature doesn't follow any rules.

It was a streak of intense protectiveness in Stanley that caused the trouble, protectiveness towards the people he loved. He'd shown it on several occasions since that day in the playground, usually to protect me and the results had often been less than pleasant — frightening, in fact. Now, in his own way, he loved Tommy's daughter.

I was still looking at Celia Gannon and I saw the compassion in her eyes cloud as she thought of something else. I knew what that was, and so did Gannon.

'Jesus Christ,' he snarled, turning to me. 'That's why you didn't want me to talk to him. The guy is a dummy. He's simple-minded.' His glare moved round to include Mrs. Jennings. 'You let a dumb-brain like this around a school full of young girls. When I've finished with this business I'll close you down.' There was a tense silence. Mrs. Jennings shifted her weight and leaned forward. She wasn't going to take Gannon lying down, but I stepped forward before she could speak. After all, it wasn't her fight.

'Shut up Gannon,' I said. 'Stanley had nothing to do with the kidnapping. If he hadn't been there the only difference would've been that he wouldn't have been hit on the head and damn near killed. They would still have got the girls. As for the safety of the children here, Stanley has never . . . .' I hesitated a split-second. I had been going to say that he had never hurt anyone, but that wasn't true. He had. But only people who were trying to hurt him, or me. I went on, 'He has never hurt anyone weaker than himself. Because he isn't clever doesn't make him dangerous. Least of all to young girls.'

'So you say,' Gannon said.

'Yes I do.' I was beginning to get angry with the man and the heavy gang sensed it and moved again, this time to line up on me.

'And so do I,' Tommy cut in. 'I've known Stanley since we were kids together and he can be with my daughter any time he wants.'

There was silence for a moment and then Parker spoke. 'Perhaps we could go into another room,' he said to me. 'Just you, me and your cousin. We can talk quietly, the three of us. It might help.' I looked at him and there was still no expression on his face. I nodded slowly. I had the feeling that Parker was a very tough man indeed, not hard like Gannon was hard, but tough. There's a difference.

But for all his toughness I didn't think he would cause any unnecessary unpleasantness.

I had crossed to the door with the dark-skinned man close behind me when the telephone began to ring.

4

As I turned back towards the desk, Parker said something softly to the man nearest the table with all the electronic equipment piled upon it. I didn't hear what was said but instantly the man reached out and pressed several switches. Then he nodded at Parker who in turn nodded at Gannon. As Gannon reached forward and picked up the telephone on the desk I glanced at the machinery on the table by the wall. The reels of the tape-recorder I'd seen brought in were spinning and some other gadgets that I didn't recognise had lit up. I knew that one of the main advantages the police possess was their ability to trace calls. I didn't think that even Gannon could manage that, despite his great wealth.

The call wasn't from the kidnappers. It was an anxious parent who had collected her daughter earlier that day and had found signs of a rash and was worried in case it was measles. With barely concealed annoyance Gannon handed the telephone to Mrs. Jennings who slid easily into her more usual role and began to placate the woman on the other end of the line. Parker nodded to me and we went out, taking Stanley into the room next door.

The dark-skinned man turned out to be careful and thoughtful, and very soon had Stanley's complete confidence. He soon compensated for the set-back caused by Gannon's attitude and, as he probed and questioned, he turned up some additional information.

First, he found that between the first blow and the second that had knocked Stanley unconscious, the engine of the Rolls Royce had started up, but there had been no sounds of any other doors opening or closing. The second snippet of information was that the scream was definitely Jenny and not Jackie. Although Stanley had said as much to me right at the start, I hadn't taken it too seriously and I'd omitted it when I'd repeated the story, not wanting to unnecessarily alarm Tommy.

'What kind of girl is Jenny Andrews?' Parker asked me.

'Intelligent, mature.'

'Compare her with Mrs. Gannon's daughter.'

'More intelligent, more mature.'

'Less likely to scream?'

'Perhaps. This is a new experience for both of them though.' I thought for a moment and then asked, 'Isn't it?'

'Yes. There hasn't been a previous attempt to kidnap Mrs. Gannon's daughter.'

I realised he had referred to Jackie in that way twice. Not by name and not as Gannon's daughter but as 'Mrs. Gannon's daughter'. I put the thought to the back of my mind. Then I realised there was something his careful questioning hadn't touched on even though my, admittedly less sophisticated, cross-examination had. I put that thought to the back of my mind too. For the moment we were all on the same side, but I wasn't certain how long that would last, especially if, as seemed likely, Gannon began to disregard the safety of Tommy's daughter.

'You said something before,' Parker said to me, 'has Stanley hurt people?'

I thought before answering. 'When things get bad he has been known to, er, lose control.'

'And I imagine that if he loses control he takes a lot of handling?'

We were both speaking softly and Stanley was watching us placidly, apparently unaware that we were talking about him. Even so I was still aware of the tension I had noticed earlier.

'You could say that,' I said.

'Your friend seems to have faith in him?'

'Yes.'

'And you do too?'

'Yes.'

Parker nodded. 'Okay, that's good enough for me. I'll go along with your judgement. Andrews seems to be a man of some character.'

'What happened in there?' I asked. 'Did he and Gannon have a set-to?'

'Yes.'

'What about?'

'The advisability of bringing in the police.'

I felt, guiltily, that I should have done something about that earlier. 'What did Tommy want to do?' I asked.

'At this stage nothing, he's happy to let things go until we have a contact.'

'And then?'

'Then he wanted to play it by ear. Call the police if the going gets rough.'

'And Gannon?'

'No police, whatever happens.'

'If the going gets really rough he won't have any choice.'

Parker looked at me bleakly. 'Don't cross him.'

'It isn't a question of anybody crossing anyone else. We all want the same thing. We want the girls back safely.'

'Maybe,' he said and I looked at him in surprise. I had formed the obvious question when we both heard the telephone ring again in the room next door. Parker went out swiftly and silently and, after telling Stanley to stay where he was, I followed.

Gannon was just picking up the telephone, the tape-recorder was running and everyone in the room tensed once more. When Gannon spoke none of us needed telling that this time it was the call we had all been waiting for.

Gannon sat, listening, his face impassive. I glanced at his wife and her expression showed clearly how bad the moment was for her. Then I saw that Lucinda was watching me and I looked directly at her. She let her eyebrows lift a fraction and then she did the tongue and lower lip routine she had done before, only this time it was deliberate, not unconscious. She didn't seem too concerned about what was happening.

I turned away without letting my expression alter. Parker was watching me, without letting his attention drift from either Gannon or the machinery that was recording what was happening on the telephone.

I began to think that Parker didn't miss very much at all.

Apart from acknowledging that he was

Carl Gannon when he first answered the telephone, the oil tycoon hadn't spoken. He didn't speak again until, obviously, the person on the line had finished. Still without speaking Gannon replaced the receiver and nodded at Parker. While one of the men wound back the tape and another spoke softly and urgently on one of the extra telephones, Parker dialled on the telephone Gannon had used and spoke quickly, in a language I didn't recognise. By the time he had finished the other man had completed his call and the tape was ready for replaying.

The voice was a man's, reedy and oddly accented. It sounded to me as if the speaker had deliberately put something into his mouth to distort his speech and the accent was there just to add to the confusion. There was also a faint but noticeable tremor that could've been part of the man's natural speech.

He started with, 'Let me speak with Carl Gannon.'

Then Gannon's voice as we had heard it. 'This is Carl Gannon speaking.'

'Listen carefully Carl Gannon. Do not

interrupt. None of this will be repeated. We have your daughter and the other girl, her friend. Neither of them will be harmed in any way just so long as you do exactly as you are told. We want money. A quarter of a million dollars. You will raise it in equal proportions of English pounds, U.S. dollars, Swiss francs and Deutschmarks. All in notes. Don't do anything foolish about marking notes or attempting to record their numbers. It would be a waste of time anyway. When the money is ready you will be told what to do with it, but you should have your private aircraft, the small one, the Beechcraft, standing by, fully fuelled and with the pilot cleared for take-off. We will call again in the morning at six o'clock precisely. Be ready for our call. We will expect a satisfactory report regarding the money.' The voice stopped and there was a click as the line was disconnected. Then there was a second click as Gannon had replaced the telephone. Then there was silence broken only when one of the musclemen leaned over and switched off the tape recorder.

There was a muffled sound from behind me and I turned round. Mrs. Gannon was holding a handkerchief to her eyes.

'For God's sake,' Gannon snarled at her. Then he looked at Parker who was watching the woman impassively. 'Well?'

Parker turned his head and looked at his employer. For a moment I thought there was, at last, an expression in his eyes, but then it was gone and I put it down to a reflection from one of the lights in the room.

'Male,' he said to Gannon. 'White, probably American.'

'He didn't have an American accent,' Gannon interrupted.

'The accent he did have wasn't anything in particular,' Parker went on as if the other man hadn't spoken. 'He said U.S. dollars, I think a European would have said American dollars. Also, when he first came onto the line he said, 'Let me speak with Carl Gannon'. A European would be more likely to say, 'Let me speak to Carl Gannon'.' He glanced at me as if for confirmation, but I don't think he really needed it. I nodded my head anyway.

'Okay,' Gannon said. One of the other telephones rang and the man nearest to it picked it up and spoke softly for a moment, then listened.

He replaced the receiver and looked at Gannon. 'The call came from the York telephone area. That is as far as they could get in the time available.'

Gannon nodded. 'They're still in this area,' he said and then glared at his wife again. 'Goddam out of the way place to have the kid educated. What the hell was wrong with London anyway?' He didn't seem to expect an answer and turned to Parker again. 'Okay, you get busy. I'll talk to Head Office.' He began to dial a number. I looked at Tommy and inclined my head at the door and went out. He followed me and we went into the room where Stanley was waiting.

'Has Jenny come back?' Stanley asked as we walked in.

'No, not yet,' I said.

'Soon,' Tommy chipped in. He looked at me. 'What do you think?'

'I don't know, but I have to admit that much as I'd like to punch Gannon on the nose he does seem to have an effective organisation. How the hell he managed to set up a wire trace on that call I can't imagine, and I'll bet the G.P.O. don't know anything about it either. At least not officially.'

'So?'

'So, even without the police, I think all that can be done is being done. At least as far as this place is concerned.'

He looked puzzled. 'Where else could something be done?'

'I'm not sure but . . . ' I broke off and glanced at my watch. 'It's midnight. They're calling back at six. That gives Gannon six hours to raise the money and do anything else he can from here. It also gives me six hours.'

'To do what?'

'I don't know, but I am supposed to be a detective.'

Tommy looked slightly embarrassed. 'Look Harry, this is big-league stuff.'

'Don't you want me to help?'

'Of course I do, damn it. It's just that,

68

well, look what they did to Stanley.' We both looked and Stanley looked back at us, a smile trying to break through the concern.

'Nobody was expecting trouble before,' I said. 'This time we are.'

'Okay Harry, but be careful.'

'I will be.'

He looked worried again. 'Do you want me with you?' From the way he asked the question I knew the answer he wanted and anyway it was the one I wanted to give him.

'No,' I said. 'You stay here. Listen to everything that goes on, watch them all the time if you can. Not the three heavy-weights. The others, Gannon, the wife, the daughter and Parker.'

'Watch them? What do you mean? You don't think there's something going on here that . . . ?'

'No I don't,' I interrupted. 'But I do think that we shouldn't assume anything. I've seen happy families and I've seen unhappy families and it's the unhappy ones that have all the troubles. The Gannon family is my idea of a very unhappy family.'

I turned to Stanley. 'Come on,' I said. 'Let's see if Mrs. Jennings can find us something to eat and then we'll go out and see what we can see.'

'Are we going to look for Jenny, Harry?'

'Yes,' I said. 'We're going to look for Jenny.'

Mrs. Jennings produced some food for us and we ate in the school kitchen and then left her there preparing food and drink for everyone else, assisted only by one of the porters, a yellowish-skinned man with too many teeth to allow him to keep his mouth closed for long and who was beginning to look a bit miffed. He was aware that something was wrong and maybe he was annoyed that nobody would tell him what it was. On the other hand maybe he didn't get paid overtime.

As we went back through the darkened building towards the front door we passed the office and I could hear voices. They were muffled, all except Gannon's. He sounded angry about something, but, as that seemed to be a normal state for him to be in, I didn't stop.

Hearing his accented voice made me think of the voice of the man on the telephone and how there had been a distinct tremor as he spoke. It might have been the way he always talked, but it seemed more likely that he was frightened.

That worried me. There is a degree of predictability about most criminals except when they are afraid of something — then they become unpredictable. And that can be another word for dangerous.

5

I drove back to the car park at the top of the cliff overlooking the long stretch of beach. I don't know what I expected to find there, if anything, least of all at one o'clock in the morning. However, I had to start somewhere and that seemed to be the only point of reference I had. I also had a thought in my mind that it might help me to prise some more information out of Stanley.

I had several unanswered, and seemingly unanswerable, questions in my mind. Some of them could only be answered by someone in Gannon's entourage and at the moment I didn't know who to approach. Parker seemed the obvious one, but I was a little worried about his failure to press Stanley on the matter of identification. At no time in his careful questioning had he asked if he had seen the faces of the man or men who had attacked him.

I could see three possible reasons for that omission. One, the least likely, was that he had forgotten to ask, two, was that he knew their faces had been masked and, three was that he already knew who they were. On reflection the last two seemed as unlikely as the first, if not more so. Still, you know what Sherlock Holmes said about that kind of thing.

Anyway, until I found an ally I could trust in the Gannon camp I was left with whatever Stanley could dredge out of his memory and the one tenuous lead that Parker had picked up. The middle-aged couple who had been on the beach.

The car park had started life as a field belonging to the farmer whose land ran along the cliff top. On one of our earlier trips to the beach with Jenny I'd got into conversation with him and he'd told me that he had begun by letting people park in the field during the summer, but he also continued using it for planting for Spring crops. Over the years the number of people using the field had grown and he had found that, by extending the period they could park there, he could increase his income from the parking fees to the point where he didn't need the winter sowing. Once that was established he decided to lay hardcore and then asphalt so that cars could use the park even when the ground underfoot was wet, a useful point on that particular part of the coast as it rained there more often than the local resorts' brochures cared to admit.

The farmhouse was about one hundred yards from the car park and, late as it was, there was still a light on. I told Stanley to sit in the car and think about what had happened. He didn't seem very happy at the idea, so I changed my mind and let him go with me to the farmhouse.

The farmer wasn't too happy either, when he came to the door, some minutes after I had knocked. He had been ready to go to bed and had stopped to pull his working trousers and jacket over his pyjamas. He'd also put his Wellingtons on and he stood in the doorway looking comically angry.

I apologised for disturbing him and told him that a little girl was missing and that she didn't know the area very well. Consequently I was looking for her in the few places she knew, and that this was one. The story sounded a bit thin, even to me, but he took it at face value and asked what he could do to help.

'When we were here earlier today there were a few other people about. I wondered if you'd seen them?'

He glanced at Stanley. 'I remember seeing him. You too, and there were two little girls, not one, on the beach. And a dog.' He sounded like a man who kept a careful watch on his property.

'That's right. I didn't see you today.'

'Ploughing in the top field. Looks right down over the cliff. Saw you there. Not many people on the beach this time of year. That's why I don't bother to collect car park fees until Spring.' I wasn't sure if that was a hint that he expected payment for his help, not that he had helped, so far.

'I'd be extremely grateful if you can remember anyone else who was here today.' I said, trying to make it sound as if gratitude meant money. 'It's always possible they've seen her since then.'

He nodded his head and stepped back from the door and waved us inside.

'Of course I'll help,' he said. 'If I can that is. This is no kind of night for a youngster to be out on her own.'

I immediately regretted my assumption that he wouldn't help without payment. 'Thank you,' I said. 'Did you see anyone else?'

'There was a big car in the car park. Rolls Royce I think. Could've been a Bentley I suppose, I was some way off.'

'Yes, I know about that car.'

There was a noise from the head of the stairs and a woman appeared and stared down at us. 'What's all this? Do you know what time it is?'

The farmer told her the reason I was there and a few minutes later she joined us, a slightly tatty dressing-gown over a thick nightdress. She seemed equally eager to help.

'I saw you,' she nodded at Stanley. 'Couldn't hardly miss you.' She smiled cheerfully at him and he managed one of his brighter smiles in return. Then she peered closely at me. 'I don't like the thought of a young girl alone out there. What are the police doing?'

I hesitated and then decided that a fairly harmless lie wouldn't go amiss at that point. 'They're looking, but I couldn't just sit and do nothing myself.'

'A relative are you?'

'Her uncle.'

That seemed to satisfy her. 'They'll find her,' she said. 'But, like you say, you can't sit and do nothing. Now, let me think.' She frowned in concentration.

'I've told him about the Rolls, but he saw that himself,' her husband put in.

'There was the van.'

'What van?' he asked her.

'Came down the road, oh, about four it would be. I remember it because I thought it was Fred Rowlands' van. I wondered what he was coming here for. But it couldn't have been him, he would've come in for a chat. It stopped near the car park and somebody got in and it went off again.'

'Did you see who got in?' I asked.

'No, just saw shapes. My eyes aren't what they were.'

'Shapes? There was more than one?'

'Yes, I'm almost sure about that. There were two of them.'

'What kind of van was it?'

'Same as Fred's, same colour.' She looked enquiringly at her husband.

'Fred has a small Bedford van. Seven hundredweight it is. Light blue.'

'That's right, light blue it was.'

'Thank you,' I said. 'Anything else? Later on, maybe. Did you see the Rolls go?' They both shook their heads. 'Well, never mind, thank you very much for all your help.'

'That's alright. Hope you find the little girl soon.'

They showed us out and stood in the doorway with the light shining over their shoulders until we'd picked our way back to the track that led down to the car park where we had left the Volvo.

Back in the car Mister Mackay insisted on sitting on Stanley's knee and I watched him absently rubbing the animal's ears with one of his big hands. I

78

decided to try him again with a few questions about the moments when the attackers had opened the car door.

'Are you sure you didn't see their faces?'

'No Harry, I don't think so.'

'Try to remember all you can. You're sure there were two of them?'

'Yes.'

'Why are you sure?'

That stopped him and he frowned as he tried to think about the events of that afternoon.

'When the door opened someone grabbed my arm. I was leaning against the door and I started to fall out of the car and I held onto the man who was holding my arm. I still had hold of him when I was hit. So there must have been another man.' He finished on a triumphant note.

'You're sure they were men? Could one of them have been a woman?'

He frowned. 'I don't think so Harry. A woman wouldn't have hit me like that would she?' I didn't answer that, there was no point in complicating his life anymore than was absolutely necessary.

'Do you think they were younger or older than we are?' I asked instead.

He thought about that too. 'Younger I think Harry. They moved quickly.' That seemed like good reasoning and part of my brain recorded the fact that he was thinking more coherently than he usually did.

I sat silently for a few minutes running over what I'd managed to conclude from the events at the school and in my conversations with Stanley, alone and with Jay Parker. There were several, seemingly trivial, odds and ends, but none of them, either separately or even together, seemed enough to build any-thing upon.

At least two people were involved, maybe more, but I didn't have a lot of hope of catching up with the middle-aged couple and even if I did there was nothing to suggest they were involved. The two were probably, not definitely, men. One of them, the man who had spoken on the telephone might be American.

As far as the events in the car park were

concerned that was still confused. If Harry's recollections were correct then Jackie, the less assured of the two girls, hadn't screamed when the kidnappers had first appeared, but Jenny had. It wasn't much, but it did give me a line of thought I wanted to pursue.

Then there was the fact that no other doors had been opened or closed on the Rolls Royce. That meant the kidnappers had got in the back, not in the front beside the driver. Alone, that didn't mean much. After all, if they were armed then a gun at the back of the head is just as effective as a gun in the ribs. But there was also the fact that Simpson appeared to have started the engine before anyone got into the car.

I decided that someone should be digging into the missing chauffeur's background. That someone had to be Parker and I guessed that he was probably doing that already, even though it seemed to be the kind of thing that should've been done when he was first employed, not now when events demanded it.

There were a couple of other things I needed to know too, but it was a problem knowing who to ask.

I realised we had been sitting there in silence for several minutes and Stanley seemed quite relaxed. I remembered a policeman acquaintance of mine once telling me about the art of interrogation. I'd listened, partly because I try not to upset the few members of the force with whom I'm on speaking terms. I decided to try one of his tricks because, even though he was talking about people who were deliberately witholding information, I couldn't see why the technique wouldn't work with someone who was trying to remember but couldn't.

'Which one hit you Stanley?' I asked casually.

'The small one,' he said. 'The one with the scar.'

I sat silent again, this time in surprise. I hadn't really expected it to work at all. Unfortunately, my surprise lost me the small advantage I'd gained because, by the time I'd recovered, Stanley had realised what he had said and was getting excited trying to remember other things which merely clouded his mind again. I managed to extract the information that the scar was beneath the right eye, but that was all he could remember.

I calmed him down and started the car. There would be other opportunities, but I felt that there was a chance that he would be able to identify at least one of his attackers. If we got that far.

I had driven about a mile towards the main road when I saw a telephone kiosk and I decided that if one long-shot had worked then it might be the night to try another. I stopped the car and went into the box and looked up the name of the man mentioned by the farmer's wife, who owned a blue Bedford van like the one she had seen come down the road and pick up two people. Fred Rowlands lived about six miles away in a village on the main coast road. It took me fifteen minutes to reach the village and locate the house.

The van was parked on the grass verge outside the cottage. I went up to the front door and knocked several times, but didn't get a reply. I left Stanley at the front of the house and went round and poked about at the back. The back door was unlocked and after a moment's thought I opened it and went in.

It opened into a small kitchen and more by touch than sight I found a box of matches on top of the gas cooker and used them to explore the ground floor. The house was shabby and in need of a lot of work. It didn't look as if Fred Rowlands had a wife, it was in desperate need of a woman's touch. I went up the stairs quickly and silently, that way they creak less than when you move slowly. There were two rooms upstairs and neither of them was a bathroom or lavatory. If the cottage had that refinement it was outside in the yard. I went through the rooms quickly with my box of matches. Nothing.

Back down stairs again I went out the way I had come in, but then I remembered I still had the matches. I didn't think they would be missed so I didn't bother to take them back, but as I still had them I thought I might as well have a look in the little row of outbuildings that sprang off the rear of the cottage. The first door was the coalshed, the second was the missing lavatory. The third was a larger, general purpose shed with a work-bench along one wall. I stumbled over something that rattled and the match went out. When I lit up again I found I had tripped over a sack, a sack full of seashells. I drew the top together again and, still holding it, I glanced under the bench. There was something there, something covered in sacking. I crouched down, lit another match and lifted the corner of the sacking.

I don't know how long I crouched there, not long probably, because a match doesn't stay lit for long, but it seemed like a lifetime.

I hadn't bothered to ask the farmer and his wife for a description of Fred Rowlands because I didn't think it was necessary. Consequently I didn't know if it was his body underneath the sacking. The chances were it was, he was old and undersized and he looked unwashed and untidy. Like his home, or rather, like his former home.

After I'd found out how he had died I dropped the sack, lit another match, and checked the rest of the outbuildings. I didn't find anything else. I had been replacing the burnt matches in the box so there was nothing to indicate I'd been there. I retraced my steps and wiped all the door handles I'd touched and then went back to the shed. Although the house was a mess the shed seemed neat and tidy. Dirty, but neat and tidy. There were tools and bits of what looked like dismantled fruit machines all arranged in neat rows. Even his body was neatly placed under the bench. All neat and tidy, except for the sack of seashells. On an impulse I picked it up and went out to where Stanley was waiting patiently by the front door.

'Nobody home,' I said. 'Let's go back to the school.'

In the car neither of us spoke until we turned into the school gates. I had been busy trying to fit the death of the little man into the other events of the past twelve hours. I didn't know what Stanley had been thinking about until he spoke as I stopped the car.

'Harry, the man who hit me. The one with the scar.'

'What about him?'

'If he hurt me he might hurt Jenny. And Jackie.'

There didn't seem any point in dissembling. 'It's possible,' I said quietly.

His huge hands clenched into fists that could be, and which, on occasions in the past, had been, used as clubs. Those occasions had often resulted in severe physical damage to individuals who, when everything was added up, had asked for it.

The massive fists relaxed and he spread his fingers, kneading them into his thighs. Even then the hands and arms looked potentially dngerous, and they were. Once, beside an underground lake in Sardinia, the hands and arms had siezed a man who had been about to kill me. They had siezed him and held him, crushed him until his ribs had smashed and pierced his internal organs, causing a massive haemorrhage that had killed him.

Apart from Stanley and I, only a couple of others knew that Stanley had killed the man and those others had nothing to gain by passing the information along. It was probably as well. I didn't like to think what the authorities would have had to say about it if they ever found out.

'We have to find them,' he said, and there was all the tension there that I'd noticed earlier. Only this time there was something stronger, a determination that was usually missing from his voice.

'We will,' I said. I tried to make it sound as if I really believed it. For the moment he seemed to accept the fact that I knew best. The trouble was, I wasn't all that sure myself. Even so I redoubled my determination to keep him with me until we found Jenny and her friend.

Then, as we went in through the front door and down the corridor towards the Principal's office I let my mind move onto other things. For the moment it seemed more important to decide who I could trust among the gathering at the school. The death of the little man had to have a relevance, but there was still doubt in my mind about the real position of Gannon's family and retainers in what was happening.

That seemed to leave Tommy, and I didn't relish the thought of telling him that murder had entered the case. I didn't relish that at all.

6

During my absence there had been no new developments. Some sandwiches had been made and coffee, but not much seemed to have been eaten.

Seeing food reminded me that I hadn't fed Mister Mackay and I went outside and let him out of the car. He tried a couple of tentative barks, listened to the echoes and then followed me up the steps into the school. I took him along to the kitchen collecting Stanley along the way and dug around until I found a tin of meat pie filling. I opened it and spooned it onto a plate and stood watching him devour it. I heard the door open and turned round. It was Celia Gannon.

I smiled at her and she tried a smile in return.

'I was hungry,' she said. 'I couldn't eat anything before but . . . ' Her voice trailed off as if she was embarrassed that at a time like this she had an appetite.

'So am I,' I told her, which wasn't true, but I thought it might help her, and it had crossed my mind that she might be the person of whom I could ask some of the questions that were bothering me.

I spent a few minutes looking through cupboards and eventually came up with slabs of fruit cake, cheese and I made some coffee to go with it.

I waited until we were sitting eating before I spoke again.

'How long has Simpson been with you?' I asked. It wasn't something I really wanted to know, but it seemed a harmless way to begin.

'About two years. The Company employs several chauffeurs. He drives Lucy, Lucinda, most of the time.'

'I would've thought she would drive herself,' I said.

'No. She doesn't have a car of her own. None of us do. Just company cars with company drivers. My husband doesn't believe . . . ' Her voice trailed off again.

'Who drives you?'

'I rarely go anywhere. If I do, one of the

91

Head Office drivers takes me, whoever is free.'

I nodded. 'What is Parker's position with your husband's company?' She shifted her position slightly and her eyes didn't meet mine.

'He is head of security.'

'The others in there, the three musclemen, they're security men I presume.'

'Them? No, they just act as bodyguards.' I wasn't too sure what the difference was between security men and bodyguards, but it didn't seem important.

'How long has Parker been with your husband?'

'Fifteen years.'

'Always as head of security?'

'No. He was a trouble-shooter in the Texas oil-fields, that's where Jay ... Parker comes from. Later, he moved up in the company.'

'Fifteen years is a long time,' I said with no particular thought in mind.

'Yes, a long time,' she said and I was surprised to see that something remarkably like a tear had formed in the corner of her eye. She stood up abruptly and walked towards the door.

'Mrs Gannon,' I said.

She stopped and turned back. 'Yes?'

'I can't pretend to offer the kind of thing your husband's clearly putting into this operation, but I want to help all I can.'

'I know and I'm very grateful.'

'That isn't why I'm telling you. I need information, information I can't get for myself.'

'Parker will tell you what you want to know,' she said.

'I didn't think he was the kind of man to break a trust.'

Her head came up sharply. 'He won't, but some things override loyalty to an inanimate thing like a company, even one like International Oil'. There was a note of bitterness in her voice that hadn't been there before.

'Will he talk to me?' I said quietly, not wanting to break the bond that seemed to have developed between us.

'I'll speak to him,' she said and stood up again and went out of the room.

I looked at the dog who had taken up a

post close to where I'd found the tin of meat.

'Well, well, well,' I said to him and he cocked an appreciative ear in my direction. I stood up and rummaged in the cupboard for another tin. I had just emptied it onto his plate and was standing, watching him wolf it down, when the door opened again. I turned round expecting Parker.

It wasn't. It was Lucinda Gannon.

She came into the room and leaned against the table, one hip jutting provocatively towards me. She flicked a glance at Stanley and then ignored him.

'I couldn't sleep,' she said.

'Couldn't you,' I said.

'What are you doing?'

'Feeding the dog.'

'Is that all?'

'Yes.'

'Is that what Celia was doing too, feeding the dog?'

I looked at her flatly. 'She wanted something to eat.'

'Did she now?' She moved away from the table and came closer to me. 'Maybe she couldn't sleep either.'

'Maybe she couldn't'

'It will take more than food to make me sleep.'

'Will it?'

'Yes.' She tried to look girlishly coy, but it didn't work. The sulky expression that had been on her face before must have been very nearly permanent and it had set her face into lines it couldn't easily shake off.

'Where are you sleeping?' I asked.

She brightened at that. 'In one of the empty dormitories. Down the corridor to the end and up the stairs to the next floor. First door on the left.'

'Perhaps it's time you went back there,' I said.

'Okay.' She seemed to read into that more than I had intended she should. She went out with some unnecessary hip-waggling and one or two over-the-shoulder glances that ought to have been sexy, but weren't.

After she had gone I went back to the office with Mister Mackey and Stanley and left them with Tommy. Nobody had moved very far. I glanced at Parker and tried to pass a message with my eyes. When I went out I waited in the corridor and a few seconds later he came out and joined me.

'What do you know about Simpson?' I asked.

'Simpson? I don't trust him although Gannon seems to.'

'How bright is he?'

'For this kind of operation, not bright enough.'

'Whoever is doing this isn't all that bright,' I said. 'At least the field staff isn't bright. I can't make up my mind about the management side.' He looked at me with more interest than he had shown before. He was about to ask a question, but I shook my head. 'First chance you get, talk to Mrs. Gannon. Then we'll talk'. I walked away before he could say anything else.

The dormitory was exactly where Lucy Gannon had said it was and so was she.

The room was large but partitioned off into small cubicles that gave the usual occupants the privacy their fee-paying parents would have expected. The partitions didn't reach to the ceiling so the privacy extended more to actions than words.

Lucinda was in bed and she had the covers pulled up around her chin. I sat on the edge of the bed and looked at her. I opened my mouth to ask the question I wanted to ask, but she reached out and put her fingers against my lips. The action allowed the sheet to drop away and I wasn't at all surprised to see that she was naked. Subtlety wasn't one of her strong points it seemed.

I stood up, retreated to a safe distance and leaned against the door. I tried to look her in the eye, but it was an effort.

'How well do you know Simpson?' I asked.

She didn't seem all that surprised by the question, just irritated. 'He drives me that's all. He isn't much of a conversationalist. I don't know anything about his background if that's what you mean.' I didn't say anything and after a moment she went on. 'It's just the kind of thing he would do. Think that this is a way to get an easy dollar.'

'You think he's involved with the kidnappers?'

She didn't answer that but shrugged her shoulders and asked a question instead. 'Don't you?'

Her breasts bounced disturbingly as she shrugged and I weakened momentarily and let my eyes drop from hers. When I pulled them back again there was a look of smug pleasure on her face that made her look more spoiled than she had at first. I didn't move from my position by the door.

'I'm not sure.' I thought for a moment. 'Do you know any of his friends?'

'Whose friends?'

'Simpson's of course.'

'Why should I?'

'No reason. I just asked.'

She thought for a moment. 'Only Curry, one of the other chauffeurs.'

'Nobody else?'

'Not that I know of.'

I nodded and turned to open the door. 'See you later,' I said.

'Bastard,' she said.

I turned and looked at her and grinned. She pulled up the sheet and glared at me angrily. I expect she felt she had cause for her opinion. I went out and closed the door quietly behind me. I waited at the top of the stairs for a few minutes until she came out of the dormitory, slamming the door noisily behind her.

She marched past me with her nose in the air. Making friends was never a strong point with me and it looked as if I hadn't broken my track record with Lucinda Gannon.

7

I went in search of Parker but as I was walking down the corridor I felt a touch on my arm. I looked round and Parker had appeared silently behind me.

'What do you want to know?' he asked.

'Several things. First though, it looks like this is an inside job.'

'Yes,' he said calmly.

I looked at him curiously. 'How did you know?'

'Later. Go on with your questions.'

'Right. It may be unnecessary now, but find out whether the call the kidnapper made to Gannon came here direct or if it was first made to somewhere else and then routed on.'

'I've already done that. It came here first. They didn't call the Gannon house and they didn't call International Oil.'

'That's what made you suspect an inside job?'

'Partly.'

I waited, but he didn't seem disposed to go on. I said, 'Sooner or later you're going to have to trust me.'

Something approaching a smile touched the corner of his mouth.

'Okay,' he said. 'Jacintha didn't scream so perhaps that was because she recognised them. Then there was the business of Simpson starting the car apparently without being told to. Add to that the fact that, apart from you and the girls, the only other person who knew that Jackie would go with you to the car park on the clifftop was Simpson. Will that do?'

It covered most of the points I'd thought of for myself. 'Yes,' I said.

'So?'

'So who put Simpson up to it?'

'You don't think he's the principal?'

'No. Do you?'

'He hasn't the brain for it.'

'Then?'

'He has a friend, another chauffeur.'

'Curry.'

'Yes. He's much brighter. Not highly intelligent, but cunning.'

'Cunning enough for this?'

'Could be.'

'Then for the moment we'd better assume that Simpson really is involved,' I concluded.

'Agreed.'

'So now we play it carefully. If we say too much at this stage we might frighten them and they're jumpy already. I don't want them any more nervous than they are now.'

'Agreed,' he said again.

'We go along with the kidnapper's demand when it comes through,' I said. 'Get back the girls and then decide what to do about Simpson and Curry later.'

'And in the meantime?'

'Whatever the ransom payment arrangements are I'm going to be involved.'

'Who says?'

'I do and Jenny's father will back me.'

'So will Jacintha's' he said firmly.

It was my turn to raise an eyebrow. 'Good,' I said. He turned to go back to the office, but I stopped him. 'There's something else.'

'What?'

'The three men in there, the body-guards, can you trust them?'

'They can be trusted to guard Mr. Gannon.'

'But that's all?'

'What are you getting at Morgan?'

'Your security people. Can you trust them?'

'With my life,' he said flatly.

'Can you get some of them over here?'

'Why?'

'There's a dead body in a cottage about four or five miles from here. It might be as well to have it removed before anyone else finds it and calls the police. It looks as if this will be wound up soon and we don't want the police muscling in at this stage in the proceedings.'

He looked at me, his face impassive. 'Where?'

I told him and he nodded and went back into the office, picked up one of the telephones and dialled and then spoke quietly for a few moments, his words inaudible to me and, I guessed, everyone else in the room.

When he replaced the receiver he

glanced at his watch. 'They said six o'clock,' he said to Gannon. 'It is almost that now.'

'There's time yet.' Gannon said. 'What was all that about?'

'Ensuring everything is under control,' Parker said. He looked at his watch again. 'They were nervous, I think they will be more nervous by now. They may call early.'

He was avoiding Gannon's question and he wasn't being as neat about it as I thought he would have been. Maybe something was troubling him. Then, before Gannon had time to pursue the point, the telephone rang.

They went through the setting up procedure as before and then Gannon picked up the telephone. Again he said little.

When the call was over and the tape was being rewound one of the musclemen made a call as before, no doubt to the tracer they had tucked away somewhere in the telephone exchange.

The voice on the tape, when it was replayed, was the same as the first time, still reedy with an odd accent and this time the nervous waver was even more apparent.

'Gannon?'

'Yes.'

'You have the money?'

'Yes.'

That surprised me and I glanced round the room and saw that one of the bodyguards was standing close to a black attaché case that stood on the floor in the corner of the room. He saw me looking at it and shifted his weight a little.

The voice on the recorder went on, 'Put it in a case. Take it yourself by car. You will follow the coast road north towards Scarborough, then take the main road to Pickering. In the middle of Snainton village there's a right turn signposted, Troutsdale. Take that road. About three and a half miles along there is a turning to the right that leads into the forest. About fifty yards from the road there is a picnic area. Stop the car there and get out. On your right you will see a table with two benches. Put the case on the table. Then go back to the car and drive back the way you came. Time it so you get there at noon. No tricks.'

Then Gannon. 'What about the girls?'

'They will be released twelve hours after we have the money. We will call you and tell you where to find them.'

'That isn't good enough . . . .'

'That is the way it will be.' The voice stopped and the telephone was disconnected. No one spoke for several moments.

Then Gannon looked at Parker. 'Set it up,' he said.

Parker nodded and went out. On the way he looked at me and I got the message and followed him.

Before I reached the door Gannon spoke again. 'Morgan, I want to talk to you.'

I turned round. 'Yes?'

'Where were you?'

I looked at him blankly. 'When?'

'For the last few hours. Where have you been?'

I thought for a moment, but could not see any reason to make it too much of a secret.

'I went to look for some trace of the couple who were on the beach.'

He frowned. 'In the middle of the night?'

'I didn't think we were clock-watching'

His frown deepened. 'You're only here on sufferance,' he said.

'No he's not.' It was Tommy joining in.

Gannon turned on him unhesitatingly. 'Keep out of this, Andrews. Your daughter is getting out of this on the back of my agreement to pay these bastards what they've asked for.'

Tommy leaned over the desk and glared at the American. 'My daughter is only in this business because of you . . . .' He broke off and turned away. His eye caught mine. 'Tell him we're all supposed to be on the same side Harry,' he said.

'That's right,' I said to Gannon. 'Let's all try to be friends for another few hours and with luck it will all be over. Then we can argue about blame and responsibility and who owes who what.'

'Don't give me orders,' Gannon snapped. I thought about having an argument with him. Then an image of

Celia Gannon's face drifted into my mind and I decided not to tussle with her husband. I had the feeling that when he found his power and wealth didn't make me hop about like his underlings, he would take it out on somebody else and that might just turn out to be her. I let out my breath slowly and grinned at Tommy.

'Don't worry mate,' I said. 'Everything will work out right in the end. For now let's go and see if we can find Mrs. Jennings and have ourselves a drink or something.'

'It's six o'clock in the morning,' he said.

'So what?' I said and he thought about that for a few moments.

'So what indeed,' he said eventually and followed me out of the office. Stanley came out with us and we went down the corridor, trying doors until we found a room that was far enough away to remove the chance of anyone overhearing us.

'Right,' I said. 'I'm taking off now. I'll take Stanley with me. We're going up to the place the kidnappers have set as the drop.'

Tommy looked worried. 'Be careful,' he said. I knew that he wasn't worried about my health. He was thinking that if the kidnappers thought they were being set up they might turn nasty with the girls.

'Don't worry,' I said. 'All I want is to be close enough to them to ensure they don't have any second thoughts when they've got the money.'

'What kind of second thoughts?'

'About trying for a bit more money,' I said.

He nodded. 'They haven't asked for much, have they?'

'No, but they're amateurs and they may be settling for a small but quick return for their efforts.' He nodded again and seemed to accept what I was saying. It wouldn't do to let him know that there was a chance that more was at stake than a quarter of a million dollars. I went on, 'Officially I'm carrying on the search for the couple on the beach, if anybody asks.'

'Okay,' he said. I turned to go, but he reached out and caught at the sleeve of my coat. 'Harry, are you sure we shouldn't have got the police in on this before now?' There was a tremor in his voice that hadn't been there before. The waiting was starting to get at him.

'No, we're doing the right thing,' I said with a lot more confidence than I felt. Then, on reflection, it seemed that maybe it really was for the best. If it turned out that all we had was a straightforward kidnapping for money, then no doubt the police would have handled it at least as well as we were doing. But if more really was involved then there was a good chance that, for all their massive resources, the police would have difficulty unravelling it. At least in the time we were likely to have at our disposal.

'I'm not finding the waiting very easy,' he said. 'Perhaps if I came with you . . . '

'No, you stay here. Keep an eye on the Gannon family and friends and see they don't do anything silly.'

'You said that before, or something like it. What do you know that you haven't told me?'

I knew I couldn't get away with telling

him the same story I'd told earlier.

'They're an odd bunch. I don't think anything will happen that's likely to prevent this thing going through alright. It's just that . . . '

'Well?'

'They seem to have more than their share of neuroses, the Gannon family that is. Under pressure they might do something unwise.'

'None of them will risk a little girl's life.'

'No, I suppose not.'

'Well then. It ever anyone had a tight grip on things, Gannon's the man. You've seen the way he talked to his wife.'

'Yes.'

'And the other daughter is a nothing. She's only interested in what men keep in their trousers.'

I grinned at him, he was sounding a bit more like himself. 'You might be right,' I said.

'Okay,' he said. 'I'll stay here, but be careful.'

'I will.'

He looked at Stanley. 'You too,' he said.

Stanley smiled at him, a beaming smile that threatened to split his cheeks. It was the first time he had been completely reassured that Tommy wasn't holding him responsible for Jenny's disappearance.

The door opened silently and Jay Parker stood in the opening.

'A word with you,' he said. Tommy looked from him to me and then went past the dark-skinned man.

'See you later Harry,' he said.

'Okay,' I said. Parker came into the room and closed the door behind him.

'The dead man. Who is he and what's his part in this?'

'His name is Fred Rowlands, he's a local man. He probably gave a lift to the middle-aged couple I saw on the beach. Apart from that, you know as much as I do.'

'Do I?'

'Just about.'

'What else is there?'

'One of the men who took the girls, the one that hit Stanley, is small and has a scar on his face, below the right eye.'

'Ah,' he said.

'Meaning?'

'That helps tie in Simpson and Curry.'

'Does it?'

'Curry would fit that description although it's a bit too vague to be certain.'

'Stanley can identify him when we catch up with him.'

'Yes,' he said. 'If we need to bother with identification.'

I looked at him, frowning. 'I'm not sure I like the sound of that.'

'Gannon doesn't want the police involved. If we get the girls back without bringing them in, then there will be the matter of dealing with the offenders.'

'He won't risk the girls' lives by doing anything foolish,' I said, remembering that the last time we'd talked about that point Parker hadn't been very certain in his answer.

'This is now a field operation,' he said. 'I am in total control of it. Gannon and the bodyguard won't get involved until it is over.'

'Good,' I said.

'What are you planning to do?'

I thought about lying, then changed my mind. 'I'm going to the forest in Troutsdale.'

'That might not be wise.'

'I'm not planning to interrupt the drop or the pick-up.'

'What are you planning to do?'

'I'm planning on protecting the kidnapper until the girls are freed.'

He nodded. 'You really don't trust Gannon, do you?'

'Do you?'

He grinned and shook his head. 'What do you think,' he said.

'Right,' I said. 'Oh, one thing, Gannon doesn't go with the money.'

'Not much chance he would.'

'Someone is taking care of Fred Rowlands' body?' I asked.

'It's already been taken care of,' he said. I was surprised and it showed. The touch of a smile came to the corner of his mouth again. 'We're efficient,' he added.

'Yes,' I said as he went out of the room.

I looked at Stanley. 'Seems a good man,' I said.

'Yes, I like him,' he paused and then

added, 'I like Mrs. Gannon too.'

I looked at him in surprise. 'You do?'

'She has a kind voice.'

I thought about that. He was right. 'Yes,' I said, 'she has. Well let's get going.' I opened the door and we went out to the car.

With Stanley driving we went out of the school and through the village. I picked a roundabout route for us, but I had already decided that the kidnappers were too amateurish to have mounted an effective lookout system.

What was worrying me was the growing conviction that although they had started off in complete control they very probably wouldn't have all that much control over forthcoming events.

8

Stanley and I had moved to Yorkshire a few months earlier and I still hadn't had time to find my way about. Tommy was due to move on from the power station site near Manchester when they reached ground level, he was a below-ground expert, a muck-shifter to use his own phrase, and the next site for him was near York. Preliminary work had already begun and Stanley was in the small crew who were operating there.

The move had suited me, because I get restless if I'm in one part of the country too long.

So, although I knew York quite well, I was a stranger to the county. The weekend trips to take Jenny out of school had helped, but I didn't know North Yorkshire and the part we were heading for was completely strange territory. From the map though, it looked as if the kidnappers had picked a very suitable place for the drop.

The road that led from Snainton village through the area known as Troutsdale ran for about seven miles with no turnings off, or at least no turnings that led anywhere other than into farms or into forest tracks and fire-breaks. At the northern end of the valley it joined a minor road that ran west, through about ten miles or so of forest until it joined the Pickering road, and east into the north end of Scarborough.

It meant that any vehicle entering Troutsdale from either end could be observed without difficulty. A trap wouldn't be easy to set. For the first time it looked as if the kidnappers were doing something less amateurish than most of their efforts. It also suggested local knowledge which brought my mind back to the dead man I had found in the cottage.

Finding a dead body is jarring at any time, but in the circumstances under which this one had turned up, it seemed particularly bad. Try as I did, I couldn't see the need for a killing. The kidnappers must have known there was a chance that Stanley would be able to identify them, but even though he had been attacked and hurt they hadn't killed him. So why kill Fred Rowlands? Which brought me to a fairly logical thought: they hadn't killed him. Someone else had done it.

It all seemed unnecessarily complicated and that bothered me, but whatever was really going on, the first priority was clear. We had to secure the return of the two girls. And that was why I was hoping to pick up the trail of whoever collected the money. I wanted to be with the collector when he returned to wherever the girls were being held. I had read enough detective stories to know that once they had the money, kidnappers had a habit of disposing of their victims in a rather abrupt and often fatal manner.

According to the map the next village to Snainton was Brompton and from there a road ran parallel to, and a couple of miles to the east of, the road into Troutsdale. This road led to the village of Sawdon and there the road stopped. I decided to go there, leave the car and cut across country to the woods that surrounded the picnic area where a few hours later someone would be making the delivery of the suitcase.

The dull, greyish weather of the previous day was being repeated and by the time we had reached Sawdon and parked the car a fine drizzle had set in and it looked as if we were going to get wet again.

We did. The distance between the village and the picnic area might have been only a couple of miles on the map, but on foot, scrambling first through fields, then the outskirts of the forest and finally the forest itself, necessitated several detours that more than trebled the distance we had to cover.

By the time we reached the eastern edge of the patch of forest that bordered the other road, it was well past ten o'clock. I stopped and squatted onto my heels and waved to Stanley to do the same.

'Is this where you think Jenny is, Harry?' he asked me as he crouched beside me.

'No, she won't be here.' Then as his face rumpled into a frown I went on. 'One of the men who took her away will be coming here. We're going to follow him.'

'Here? One of them is coming here?'

'Yes.' I said, and when he didn't say anything more I looked at him carefully. Beneath the bandage on his forehead his face was set and unsmiling. He hadn't smiled a lot since the attack on him the previous day. In another man that would have been natural, in Stanley it wasn't. Most of the time he smiled whether or not there was anything to smile about.

I glanced down at his hands. They were clenched into tight balls again, I looked up from them to his face. He was looking at me. 'What's happening Harry?' he asked quietly.

I thought for a moment. There didn't seem very much point in pretending that I knew exactly what was happening or that all would necessarily work out right in the end. He knew the girls had been kidnapped; he knew the men who had taken them were violent, at least they had been towards him; and he'd heard enough of the conversations in the office at the school to know that a ranson had been demanded and was being paid that day.

I told him everything that was going on, both known and suspected, but, needless to say, I missed out the fact that Fred Rowlands had been killed. When I'd finished I wasn't sure how much he'd understood, perhaps most of it, perhaps only some of it.

I glanced at my watch, the courier would have left the school and would be on his way to the drop point. 'Come on let's go.' I moved off through the dripping trees with wet undergrowth slapping against my legs. It crossed my mind that maybe I should have told Stanley about my plans earlier. His uncomplicated view of life and people might have given me a different angle on things.

9

Most of the trees in the forest were coniferous and consequently provided good cover for us. We took it slowly because it wasn't easy, and stopped every couple of hundred yards to listen and look to ensure we were not being observed.

As far as was possible we made very little noise although Stanley, whose bulk was balanced by a lightness of movement I envied, was better at moving quietly than I was. He was also more observant than me.

'Harry. There's someone there.' His voice was soft and I stopped and followed his pointing finger. For a few seconds I couldn't make out what he had seen, but then I saw the man. He was too far off for me to identify him and there was no chance, at that range, to know whether or not he was armed. I assumed he was. It was not time to start taking chances.

Beyond the man the trees thinned a little and by manouevering myself into a position from where I could overlook his field of vision I eventually made out the picnic area. The tables and benches were heavy, rough-hewn timber affairs and, given the right weather, probably made a pleasant place to sit and relax and forget your cares. It was a nice thought.

'You stay here,' I whispered. 'I'm going a little closer.'

Stanley nodded. 'Okay Harry.'

I eased my way forward until I had halved the original distance. Then I decided not to risk my luck any more and I settled down into a fairly comfortable position and glanced at my watch. There was still a long wait ahead.

I saw the car before I heard it. It was on the road and just slowing down to turn onto the track that led into the trees. I glanced quickly behind me to ensure that Stanley was keeping out of sight. I had a momentary feeling of unease when I couldn't see him, but then I saw a bush move and he cautiously waved a hand at me. I turned back to see what the other man was doing. He was quite still, watching the car which, by then, had stopped. After a moment the door opened and a man climbed out. From my range it looked like Gannon and it seemed as if Parker hadn't managed to persuade his employer to make the switch I had suggested. Then the figure reached into the car and lifted out the case I had seen in the office at the school and walked across to the table. The walk was unlike Gannon's slightly aggressive manner and there was none of the long arm swing I had noticed before. He was wearing a hat and a scarf and had his coat collar turned up high and it could really have been anyone.

I watched intently to see if there was any attempt by the man with the case to signal to the man he must have known was waiting and watching in the woods. I saw nothing that could have been a sign.

After standing the case on the table the man turned and walked back to the car, climbed in and moments later it reversed along the track towards the road. Long before it had disappeared from sight the man in the trees began to move forward to the table. He picked up the case and I tensed, not knowing which way he would go. To my surprise, and alarm, he started back towards where I was crouched in the undergrowth.

Then, just before he reached the place where I was hiding, he turned off to his right and began to quicken his pace. From the ease with which he moved I guessed there was a path he was following.

Cautiously I moved off, keeping pace with him, but well back and still among the trees. I kept checking behind me to where Stanley had been, but again I couldn't see him.

Then, suddenly and clearly, behind me, there was a sharp, echoing crack. I stopped and the man I was following stopped. Behind me I heard the sound again. I didn't turn, but I guessed it was Stanley being less light on his feet than he usually was.

The man I was watching spun back to face the direction the sound had come from and then he turned back and began to run. I scrambled along as best I could and then realised I was losing him and that now he was running he was no longer likely to hear me if I got closer to him. I changed direction and went down onto the path he was using and began to run. Without the encumbrance of a suitcase I soon began to gain on him.

I heard footsteps behind me and turned my head and saw Stanley was closing up on me and, at that same moment, my ankle gave way and I went sprawling forward onto my face. I felt Stanley pick me up and I tried to move forward again, but my ankle wouldn't take my weight.

'Follow him,' I said. 'But for God's sake don't get too close. And don't try to do anything. Just see where he goes and then come back for me.'

He nodded and took off down the path, his long legs eating up the distance the man with the case had put between us.

I tried hopping along after them and then gave up after I'd fallen onto my knees twice more. I looked around me and a little way along the path I saw a dead or dying tree and managed to reach it and break off a branch. Then, using it as a makeshift crutch, I hobbled along the path. After a couple of hundred yards the track forked, one path climbing up and one dropping down towards where I knew the Troutsdale road lay. I stopped and listened. I couldn't hear anything. I tossed a mental coin and turned right onto the path that went downhill. It seemed a good possibility as it was the quickest way to the road.

I reached the Troutsdale road and there was no sign of anyone or anything. I'd guessed wrong. I stood at the road-side trying to decide what to do when I heard a vehicle coming along. I turned round and waited for it to come into view. It was a Landrover and when it stopped I recognised the driver. It was Jay Parker.

'What happened?' he asked as he leaned through the window.

'Open the door,' I said. I hobbled round the front of the vehicle and clambered aboard. 'The drop and the pick-up went okay, but he heard us and took fright.'

'So we lose,' he said.

'Maybe not. Stanley is following the man who picked up the money.'

'Stanley?' There was doubt in his voice.

'He'll do his best. He wants Jenny back as much as any of us.'

Parker grunted, then he asked, 'What happened to your leg?'

'I twisted my ankle.'

'What arrangements did you make to meet up with Stanley?'

'The car is in the next village, over the hill there. He'll go back there.' I hoped I sounded more confident than I felt.

Ten minutes later my confidence had sunk to an all-time low.

As we drove into Sawdon the windscreen had steamed up on the inside and I leaned forward and wiped it clear with my sleeve and peered out as we reached the place where we had left the Volvo.

It wasn't there.

10

We went back to the school. It wasn't the course of action either of us wanted to follow, but there didn't seem to be any choice. We had no idea where Stanley had gone. It was a reasonable assumption that the man he had been following had taken the left-hand fork in the path through the forest. The chances were that it was an easier, quicker, route, between Sawdon and the picnic area than the one Stanley and I had taken. A further assumption was that he'd had a car there and had gone off in it and Stanley had followed. It was logical and we didn't have any other possibilities. It didn't make it any more palatable.

When we reached the school I was in a far from happy state of mind and I wasn't looking forward to explaining to Tommy, and to Gannon, what had gone wrong with the plans that had been made for us by the kidnappers. To say nothing of what had gone wrong with the alternative plans I had instigated myself.

I was also cold, wet and tired from almost thirty-six hours without sleep. And my ankle hurt like hell.

At the school I let Parker tell his boss and Tommy what had happened while I went in search of the nurse and got her to strap up my ankle after first poking and manipulating it in a manner that made me yell, but which seemed to satisfy her that it was a sprain and not a fracture.

By the time I got back to the office everyone had had time to get themselves thoroughly depressed.

'Sorry Tommy,' I said. 'It didn't work out quite as I'd hoped.'

'It could've been worse. If you hadn't gone we wouldn't be any further ahead and as it is there's a chance Stanley might find where the man was heading.' He didn't sound convinced.

I looked around the room. There were six of us there, seven if you counted Mister Mackay who was lying under the leather couch, his eyes closed, but his ears twitching in case he missed anything. The six were Tommy, Parker, Gannon, me and two of the bodyguards.

'Where are Mrs. Gannon and Lucy?' I asked.

'Lucinda,' Gannon corrected.

'Lucinda,' I agreed.

'Mrs. Gannon is bathing and Miss Gannon is resting.' Again it was Parker who provided the answers.

'Alone?'

'What the hell do you mean?' It was Gannon again, his beaky nose homing in on me like a rifle barrel.

'I mean is anyone guarding them?'

'You think . . . ' Gannon started to speak and then turned to Parker. 'Are they alone?'

'They're covered,' Parker said quietly.

Gannon looked back at me, then at Parker and then back at me again. He didn't seem very happy.

'Let me tell you what I think,' I said. 'I think this has been an inside job. The kidnapping, the ransom demand, everything.' I hesitated and thought about the dead man I had found in the cottage. 'Almost everything,' I amended.

'Probably Simpson and another chauffeur.' I paused and looked enquiringly at Parker who reminded me of Curry's name. 'Plus one other man.'

Gannon looked at Parker. 'Do you go along with this?' he asked.

'For the moment.'

'Okay,' Gannon said to me. 'So the kidnapping was an inside job, it was certainly done amateurishly and the ransom demand was too small to make it likely any big-time operators were involved.'

I suppose he was right. Mind you, his idea of what was a small amount of money wasn't everybody's. I had no hard evidence to support my guesswork, but it seemed almost certain that Simpson was involved. Simpson and probably Curry and one other, and, as far as I could see, none of them had a reason for killing Fred Rowlands.

My stumbling brainwork received a welcome interruption when the door opened and Celia Gannon came into the room. She saw my slightly dishevelled appearance.

'What happened?' she asked.

'Things didn't go well.'

'The girls?' Her voice was strained.

'Nothing to worry about,' I said not very convincingly. 'They've got the money and there's a chance that Stanley will find out where they're holding the girls.'

She didn't say anything at that, but her face said what was in her mind. I couldn't blame her for thinking the way she obviously was doing. I trust Stanley in most things, but keeping tabs on a kidnap gang, when the safety of the victims is at stake, is a bit beyond the kind of things he usually gets to do alone.

'Cropton Forest,' she said suddenly. We all looked at her. 'Is that far from where you took the money?'

'Why?' Gannon asked.

'There are some cabins there, holiday cabins. I had a brochure about them, oh, a long time ago.'

'So?' Gannon sounded what I now took to be his usual irritable self.

'I talked about it to Simpson one day. I asked him if he knew the area and he said he did.'

'How long ago was this?' I asked.

'Ages. Well over a year.'

I thought for a moment, trying to conjure up a mental picture of a map of the area.

'Is it near?' Celia Gannon asked.

'Not far.'

'How long by car?' Parker asked.

'Half an hour.' We looked at one another.

'It's possible,' he said.

'An outside chance.'

'Better than sitting here doing nothing,' he said getting up and leaving the office.

'I don't . . . ' I said following.

'I have a feeling,' he interrupted, pausing outside the office door.

'A sixth sense doesn't make evidence.'

'Maybe not but I've learned to follow my instincts.'

'So do I,' I said. 'At the moment I haven't any.'

'I have,' he said firmly. I shrugged, but he didn't notice and went on speaking.

'One of my great-grandparents was a Chiricahua.' He was silent for a moment. Then he added, 'Sometimes I wish there was more of that blood in me.'

'Why?'

'You don't know the way Gannon operates. If there was more Chiricahua in me then maybe I wouldn't be where I am, doing the things I do.'

'Nobody's forced to do things they don't want to do,' I said.

He stopped and looked at me. 'You don't believe that, Morgan. Do you do what you want to do? Do you look after your cousin Stanley because you want to or because you have to?' He paused to let me answer. I didn't.

There was something about the turn in the conversation that sounded like something I didn't want to think about. Most of the time I soldier on without too much introspection. It makes life a lot easier, or at least it does for me. But he was right of course. I didn't look after Stanley because I wanted to, I did it because I had to. As a result my life was one of perpetual responsibility for another human being. I've sensed that a lot of people with children tolerate the problems and restrictions of bringing up a family because inside, either consciously or subconsciously, they know that the tunnel they're in has an end to it. My tunnel didn't have an end to it. There was no reason why Stanley wouldn't live as long as me, longer even.

Just then Tommy came out of the office.

'Time I did something,' he said.

The three of us climbed into Parker's Landrover and we drove off. There wasn't much conversation, but then, none of us had very much to say.

11

Parker drove fast, following the instructions I gave him as I studied a map in the light of a torch.

The Landrover was equipped with a radio and he had left a request with Gannon that someone, somehow, should trace the exact location of the cabins and relay the information on to us.

We were almost on the edge of Cropton Forest before the call came and I tied in what was said with what I could see on my map.

We stopped well short of their exact location and went in the rest of the way on foot.

The holiday cabins were nothing like I had imagined them to be. I expected a few thrown-together, pre-fabricated huts, but they turned out to be solidly built, large detached timber houses that looked more like something from a holiday advertisement for Canada than part of the landscape of North Yorkshire.

Parker told Tommy and I to stay where we were and he floated off into the darkness, his movements soundless on the soft ground.

He was away about five minutes and when he came back he was standing about a foot from my left ear before I heard him. Somehow I managed to stop myself from yelling when he touched my arm.

He pointed off into the darkness. 'There's a row of cabins, seems as if there's candlelight in one of them. There're no lights in any of the others.'

'Chances are none of them are in use at this time of the year. Power's probably been cut off at the mains,' I said.

'Right.'

'So what do we do?' I asked.

'I'll go down to the far end and work my way backwards checking each cabin in turn. You wait here.' He stopped speaking and disappeared as silently as he had materialised earlier. It occurred to me that Jay Parker was a lot closer to his great-grandparents than he seemed to think he was.

'I'm bloody glad he's on our side,' Tommy said echoing my thoughts.

'Tommy . . . ' I started to say, but he must have read what I was going to say from the tone of my voice in that one word.

'I know what we're likely to find when we get into the right cabin,' he said. 'I'm just not thinking about it, that's all.'

I hadn't time to say anything in reply, even if there had been anything to say that wouldn't have been completely ineffectual. We both heard the noise in the trees and simultaneously we spun round and moved forward like a well-rehearsed team. It crossed my mind that there might be a couple of things we could do as well as Parker, but then everything else went out of my mind as I recognised the massive figure that loomed out of the trees.

Stanley saw us at the same moment and even in the strange circumstances of our reunion I half expected his usual broad, welcoming smile. I didn't get it.

'What's . . . ?' I started to ask, but it

wasn't my night for finishing sentences.

'Harry, they've gone. They're not here.'

'Okay Stanley,' I said. 'Take it easy. Start at the beginning.'

He did, but before he managed to get halfway through Jay Parker reappeared and filled in the details of what seemed to have happened in one of the cabins.

We all went in there and it wasn't very difficult to imagine the scenes of the past few hours.

The man Stanley had followed through the woods after I had twisted my ankle had found a quicker, easier route to Sawdon, as I'd guessed he might. His car was there and when he drove off Stanley had followed in the Volvo.

Apparently the alarm the man had shown when he heard us behind him had transmitted itself to his driving and Stanley had had a hard time keeping up with him. Eventually the car had stopped elsewhere in Cropton Forest and, with Stanley close behind him, the man had headed into the woods. Then, although a very silent mover for such a big man, Stanley had stumbled and made a noise and the man had heard him. He had panicked and started shooting.

Stanley faltered there, in the telling of what had happened next, but from what he said I could easily imagine the scene.

The shots hadn't frightened him, quite the reverse in fact. They had angered him and all the pent-up distress at the loss of the two little girls had burst out of him.

He had charged forward through the trees, heedless of the noise he was making and heedless too of the bullets that whistled past him snapping into branches and tree trunks. He had reached the gunman and, sweeping him off his feet, had carried him backwards into the undergrowth.

He didn't know what had happened to the gun but there had been no more shots. Perhaps all the bullets had gone, perhaps it had just dropped in the panic the man must have felt. In any event he had been defenceless against the immense strength Stanley brought to bear on him as he crushed him to his chest.

Then, from somewhere in the back of Stanley's mind, he had heard my voice, not talking to him but shouting at him as I had done on other occasions when he had been in a rage and had gripped a man the way he was gripping that one.

Abruptly he had hurled the man away from him into the trees. Amazingly the man had been able to run — probably through fear more than anything — and he disappeared among the trees. Then, after only a moment, Stanley had cooled sufficiently to remember that he was supposed to be following the man for me and he had followed.

This time, without any attempt to conceal the direction in which he was heading, the man had gone straight to one of the cabins. Perhaps he had hoped that one of his partners would protect him.

Whatever his reason he had plunged into the cabin and there had been a single shot. Stanley had run forward and burst in through the door. He had heard someone going out of the other door and he had paused long enough to take in the scene in the room, dimly lit as it was by the light from two candles. Then he had left, through the other door and had followed the man through the forest. At the time he had thought he was still following the same man. He wasn't.

Eventually he had lost the man and had returned to the cabin, hoping to find what wasn't there.

There were two bodies in the cabin. One was Curry, the man with a scar on his cheek who had carried the case containing the ransom money. His clothing was torn and his face and hands were scratched from his flight from Stanley. By some miracle of tenaciousness he still had the case. Then I saw that it was fastened to his wrist by a loop of thread, he must have done that as a precaution when he was walking through the dark forest.

The other man was tall and despite his soiled, casual clothing, looked well-groomed.

We took a slow and careful inventory of the cabin. There were obvious signs that someone had been held there. Ordinary bandages, but cut through when someone had released whoever had been bound with them.

There were the remains of hastily prepared meals, cold food only, as we had guessed there was no electricity and although there were gas cylinder cooking facilities, no attempt had been made to use them. The occupants hadn't wanted to attract the attention of forestry workers.

Parker opened the case. The money was intact.

We looked closely at the two bodies. Both had been shot in the back. As far as a cursory examination could tell us, the shot that had killed Curry had been at close range; there was some singeing of the material of his coat around the area where the bullet had entered the body. There were no similar markings around the hole in the back of the other man's thick, fur-lined jacket. That was about as far as we could take things. From then on, any details were a matter for experts with microscopes and the like. That indirect thought about the police didn't seem to help my mind to grasp the new state of affairs that had descended on us.

'We'd better go back,' Parker said

quietly, after we had all fallen silent again.

'How far is it from here to where you left the car?' I asked Stanley. He told me and it was too far for my dodgy ankle. I asked Tommy if he would go with Stanley and bring it round to the place where we had left the Landrover. 'You go back to the school,' I said to Parker. 'Tell them what we found here.'

'What did we find here?' he asked quietly.

I looked around the spacious living room of the cabin. 'I'm damned if I know,' I said.

He nodded as if that concurred with his own thinking.

'What about this lot?' I asked.

'Someone will tidy up,' Parker said as if he arranged that kind of thing all the time. I recalled his remark about working for Gannon and the implied comment that what he did wasn't always very pleasant. Maybe he really did do that kind of thing all the time.

'We can't go on keeping this from the police,' I said. 'Three dead men, two kidnapped young girls, to say nothing of an unreported ransom demand.'

'It's too late to bring them in now,' he said. 'With what we've concealed from them so far they could put all of us away for longer than any of us would like.' He was right, so I didn't argue.

'Okay,' I said. He nodded and went out.

I dropped into one of the comfortable armchairs and waited.

By the time Tommy returned to tell me they had brought the Volvo round to where I could reach it without too much strain on my ankle, I had begun to feel quite rested. The cabin was very pleasant and comfortable.

I hadn't formed any conclusions though, my brain didn't seem to want to function in the presence of the two bodies.

It didn't function very well after we were outside either although I exercised it all the way back to the school.

12

Parker had reported the basic facts to Gannon, who was still in the Principal's office and looked as if he hadn't moved since we had left. There was a difference however, he was alone. The musclemen were outside, one in the corridor and another outside the window in the grounds.

We trooped in, Tommy, Stanley and I and sat down in a heavy silence.

'You've screwed up,' Gannon said flatly.

'No,' Parker said. I looked at him curiously. I still hadn't worked out the rather odd relationship that seemed to exist between the two men. 'We've been second all the way along the line.' Parker went on. 'Right from the off. The man and woman on the beach. It has to be them, among others probably. They've been in the chase before any of us even knew there was a chase to be in.'

'Go on,' Gannon said.

'We make a guess here,' I said, deciding it was time to prove I wasn't there just to make up the number. 'For some reason the couple didn't use a car of their own. They were picked up by a local man in a van. Maybe they needed him for local knowledge, I don't know, but what I do know is that at some point in the proceedings he either got in their way, or they decided they had no further use for him.' I paused, not for effect, but because I wasn't sure how Tommy and Gannon would react to the knowledge that I'd kept something important from them. 'They killed him.'

'How long have you known that?' Tommy asked.

'I'm sorry mate,' I said. 'I didn't think it was something you needed to know.'

He nodded acceptance of that, but Gannon didn't like it. 'You take too much on yourself Morgan,' he said.

'I knew,' Parker said.

Gannon glared at him. 'The same applies to you,' he said.

'How did he die?' Tommy asked me.

'Same as the others. Shot in the back.'

'What the hell is going on?' Gannon asked.

'We're still guessing, but it looks as if the second gang, whoever they are, got wind of what Simpson and the others were up to and followed along at a safe distance. They let them carry out the kidnapping, then they followed them to the cabin in Cropton Forest. One of them must have stayed there while the other, or others, took Fred Rowlands' body back in his van and dumped both at his cottage.

'The one who stayed behind killed the tall man and took the girls. He probably put them in the Rolls, we still haven't found that, left them there and then went back to wait for Curry, shooting him as he arrived at the cabin.'

'Why?'

'They wanted the money. There was a quarter of a million in the case. There was no point in leaving that behind and as far as they were concerned there wasn't much risk. But then Stanley appeared on the scene and our unknown friend couldn't risk the chance that he was alone and unarmed. He decided not to push his luck and took off.'

'So that's what happened,' Gannon said.

'It fits.'

'It's all wrapped up neatly but it doesn't get us beyond the original problem,' Parker said.

'The girls,' I said.

'The girls,' he agreed.

'There's still Simpson,' Tommy put in. 'Could he have done it? Killed the others I mean.'

Parker shook his head. 'I doubt it.'

'Then where is he?'

'The chances are he's somewhere in the forest. Hiding, if he was lucky and if he wasn't lucky then he'll be dead like the others.'

I stood up and gestured to Stanley to follow me. I walked to the door and as I did so I reached out and rested my hand on Parker's arm.

'Come on,' I said. 'Let's get something to eat.' He didn't answer and with surprise I realised that his arm was shaking. Not a violent shake, just a tremor. I looked at his face, but it was its usual expressionless mask. 'Come on,' I said again and after a moment his eyes focussed on mine.

He nodded his head. 'Right,' he said tonelessly.

We went out into the corridor and when the door was closed I said to him, 'Do you want to talk?'

He glanced at the bodyguard. 'No,' he said.

I watched him walk away down the corridor and looked at my watch. It was midnight.

'Come on Stanley,' I said. 'Let's go and see if those mattresses are still on the gymnasium floor.'

We walked down the corridor, Stanley silent and my mind elsewhere. In the distance I could hear a dog barking.

'Sounds like Mister Mackay,' I said. 'You go on, I'll go and find him.'

'Alright Harry,' he said, his voice subdued.

I looked at him quickly. I hadn't given much thought to how he was taking things. 'Are you okay?' I asked.

He nodded slowly. 'Are we ever going

to see Jenny again?' he asked.

'Of course we are,' I said.

'When?'

'Soon.'

'You don't know that,' he said. 'You're just saying it.' He walked on down the corridor leaving me standing with my mouth hanging open. Not for the first time since it had all begun it looked as if my judgement about Stanley was wrong. After forty years of knowing his every move, often before he knew himself, it looked as if I still had a lot to learn. It was an odd feeling.

Then I shrugged my shoulders. It would all seem better after a few hours sleep I told myself and went in search of the dog.

13

I woke up feeling as if I'd been run over by a truck. For the first few seconds I had the impression it was still on top of me, but then, as consciousness returned, I managed to sit up without breaking anything and tried to work out what it was that had woken me.

I had found Mister Mackay in the school's main hall, charging around in the darkness with his tail in the mouse-hunting position. I had taken him back to the gymnasium where Stanley was already asleep and within seconds I was fast asleep myself.

It seemed like a year ago, but when I looked at my watch it was only four hours. I realised that it was the dog that had woken me. It was scratching at a door in the corner of the gymnasium and I stood up, walked over and let it out. The door opened into the grounds and Mister Mackay disappeared into the bushes to do what well-trained dogs are supposed to do in bushes.

I didn't feel a lot better for my four hours sleep, but I knew that the chances of going back to sleep again were a bit remote and I came to the conclusion that a cup of tea would do more for me than anything else at that moment. I left the door open, hoping that the school's central heating would offset the inrush of cold air and went back across to the other end of the gymnasium, checked that Stanley was still asleep, which he was, and went out and along the corridor to the kitchen. I made myself a cup of coffee and sat there, staring at the table top, trying to decide what I'd got. It wasn't much.

That the man and woman had been picked up by Fred Rowlands in his van was the only lead I seemed to have. I went back to Mrs. Jennings' office and pushed open the door. Tommy was laid out on the leather settee and Gannon was sitting at the desk, a telephone in his hand. He looked up as I came in and I sat down in one of the other chairs and waited.

After a minute or so during which he didn't speak but was obviously listening he said, 'Right,' and replaced the receiver. 'Well?' he asked me.

'As far as I can see we've got two places to start digging. One is a straight follow-up on the man and woman I saw on the beach. That's routine detective work and I'll get onto it shortly.'

'It isn't routine for you,' he said. 'You've no standing and no facilities.'

'I've got a brain and a tongue,' I said.

He didn't reply to that, but I got the feeling he wasn't too impressed with my assets. Instead he said, 'Add to that you haven't got a personal involvement.'

I glanced at Tommy who was fast asleep. 'I think I have,' I said.

'Tell me,' Gannon said, but he was really saying, convince me.

I told him a little about the three of us, Tommy and Stanley and I, and our lives together as kids, and the problems Tommy and I had shared over Stanley, and then I came onto Jenny and how the fact that I was an unwilling child-minder didn't diminish the sense of responsibility

I felt at her being kidnapped when she was supposed to be in my care.

He nodded when I'd finished. I replayed what I'd said in my mind and it sounded to me as if I was more concerned at the slur on my ability to look after someone placed in my care than I was at the fact that Tommy and I were old friends. Maybe that's what he had heard in my voice and it was very probably why he seemed prepared to accept my continued involvement without any more argument. It was more understandable to him that I cared about my reputation than that I cared about my friends.

'Okay,' he said. 'Do what you can, talk to Parker, he'll back you up. You said there were two places to start digging. What is the other?'

'Among Jackie's friends.'

'What?' It was the first time since I'd met him that Gannon had shown any surprise.

'I don't know anything about girls' schools,' I said. 'This is the only one I've ever been in, but I imagine it's pretty difficult to keep secrets in a place like this. Maybe some of the girls know something that will help. It's a small chance but at least we can ask a few questions.'

'How? The place is almost empty.'

'We ask those that are here and as the others start to come back we ask them. The time for them to return from their weekend break is four this afternoon. We pick them out as they come in.'

'How do we know which ones to pick out?'

'The girls in the same class or dormitory. Plus any close friends not in their class.'

'Okay. I'll talk to Mrs. Jennings.'

'Right.' I stood up. 'I'll make a start on the trail of the man and woman on the beach.'

I reached the door before Tommy spoke. 'Harry.'

I turned round. 'Yes?'

'These people have killed three men.'

'I know.'

'You don't carry a gun,' he said because he knew I didn't.

'You don't?' Gannon said because he seemed to think I did.

'No.'

'Don't you think you should be armed?'

'Not me. I wouldn't know what to do with one. I'd probably shoot my own foot off.'

'You know best,' Tommy said. 'Just be careful.'

'Don't worry,' I said. I looked at Gannon who clearly didn't think I did know best and was worrying.

'What do I do?' Gannon asked. I wondered, fleetingly, how long it was since he had asked anyone a question like that.

'You wait for the telephone call.'

'What telephone call?'

'The one from the new kidnappers. The one asking for the new ransom. Only this time there's a difference.'

'What?'

'I want both girls on the telephone, Jackie to talk to you and Jenny to talk to her father. If the kidnappers object to a long conversation for fear you'll trace the call, then tell them to make two or more separate, short calls, but get both girls on the 'phone and see that everything they say is recorded.'

'What if they refuse?'

'Tell them no money unless you have proof both girls are alive.'

Gannon's eyes narrowed and I looked at Tommy who was looking intently at me. 'I have no doubts they're alive,' I said. I almost added, now, but that sounded as if I wasn't sure they would remain that way. 'What I want is to give the girls a chance to try to tell us something. A message of some kind, something we can use to trace them. Particularly Jenny.' I looked at Tommy carefully. 'Ask her if she has a message for me. She knows I'm here and involved and she knows I'm a detective. She's smart and she might get something across to us.'

'Okay,' Tommy said. I looked at Gannon and he nodded.

I went out of the office and stood outside the door for a moment, thinking. I had tried to give them both a feeling that everything was under control and would work out according to plan. I wished I had convinced myself.

Parker stopped me near the front door. 'I'll talk to the farmer,' he said.

'Why?'

'You can't do everything. Anyway, I have to do something.'

I looked at him for a moment. There was a note of urgency in his voice that hadn't been there before.

I nodded my head. 'Okay,' I said. I stood in the open doorway and watched him go. Then I went back to the gymnasium for Stanley and found that the dog was missing again. I stuck my head in the office and told Tommy to look for his dog himself. A lost dog was something I couldn't cope with on top of everything else.

After that there was nothing to do but go out into the dirty grey of the early morning and try to walk some fresh air and ideas into my brain.

14

'Harry.' Stanley broke into my thoughts as we walked briskly along the road away from the school.

'Yes?'

'Will they blame me if Jenny and her friend don't come back?'

I looked sideways at him. His face was set in a frown that had become almost as much a part of him in the past few hours as his usual wide smile had been for the rest of his life.

'Of course not, I've told you that already.' I'd got the wrong tone of voice. I sounded angry with him, even to my own ears.

'You blame me,' he said simply.

'No,' I said. 'I'm sorry, I shouldn't have snapped at you. Look, what happened would have happened whoever was there. If I'd been there they would've laid me out as well. Whoever'd been there it would have ended the same. They had it planned and you and I were unimportant.'

He didn't speak for a few moments during which time I continued with my train of thought.

'If they hurt Jenny . . . ' Stanley started to say, but I recognised the sound in his voice and interrupted hastily.

'Listen Stanley. Don't do anything to anyone. Whatever happens. Understand. Leave it all to me. This is something I can handle and jumping in and attacking these people isn't going to help the girls.' Always supposing we get close enough, I thought.

'Alright Harry. I'll do as you say,' he said reluctantly.

We walked on in silence. I knew he meant what he had said. The trouble was, if it looked as if the kidnappers really meant to harm the girls and Stanley got to know of it, any promise made to me would be forgotten. Not deliberately, but in the heat of the moment it would disappear from his mind as if it had never been there.

We walked back to the school and I

headed for the Principal's office. Before I reached it I saw the Principal herself coming along the corridor towards me.

'Hello Mrs. Jennings,' I said.

'Mr. Morgan. Have you any news?'

'Nothing I'm afraid.'

'Oh dear. It really is most distressing.'

I wasn't too sure how much she knew about the killings and although she looked as if she was capable of withstanding any shock I could throw at her, there didn't seem much point in spreading alarm and despondency.

Instead I said, 'Has Mr. Gannon told you we would like to talk to Jenny's and Jacintha's friends when they come back later today?'

'Yes, he has. A good idea too, I think. There are very few secrets in a place like this. It may well be that someone knows something that will be of use to you.'

'Let's hope so. Four o'clock is the deadline isn't it?'

'Yes. The first arrivals are usually here by about three-thirty. I'll make up a list of the girls in their class. The same girls also share the same dormitory and, as far as I

163

know, they have few friends outside the class.'

'All of them are away? None of their classmates are among the pupils who didn't go home for the weekend?'

'No.'

'Right. Could you be around when we talk to them? It will be easier I think.'

'Yes, of course.'

'Perhaps there is somewhere else we could work, using your office like this can't be very convenient?'

'No, stay where you are. I will use the general office for the time being.'

'How will you explain our presence to your staff, and the girls for that matter?'

'I will tell the staff that you are here to discuss expansion of the school's teaching facilities by use of electronic teaching aids. That will account for the tape recorders and other devices Mr. Gannon has installed in my office.'

That wouldn't account for all the very unscholastic-looking people filling her office, but I couldn't think of anything better.

'What about the girls?'

'It will be best not to tell them anything, in any event it isn't my practice to keep pupils informed of administrative actions.'

'Fine. If your staff recognise Mr. Gannon, as I expect they will, you could tell them he is thinking of endowing the school with the financial wherewithal to enable you to install the electronic aids.'

Mrs Jennings smiled thinly. 'A good idea Mr. Morgan. I'll do that.'

I left her and went on into the office.

'They've called,' Tommy said as soon as I opened the door.

'When?'

'Half an hour ago.'

'And?'

'I'll play it back,' Gannon said.

There were six of us in the room. The others were Jay Parker, Celia Gannon and one of Gannon's bodyguards.

After Gannon had identified himself on the telephone the other voice made a short statement. The voice was that of a man, not young, but not wavery. Although it was probably putting two and one together to make four it seemed a reasonable assumption that it was the male half of the couple I had seen on the beach. There was something stilted about his speech and I guessed that what he said had been written down to ensure that he made no inadvertent comments that might give something away.

He said, 'We have the two girls. You know from other events that we will not hesitate to take extreme action should you make it necessary. No police contact shall be made. If the police become involved, through no fault of yours, we shall still negotiate, but all figures mentioned will be doubled. Do you understand so far?'

Then Gannon's voice. 'Yes.'

'The sum required for their safe return will be two million dollars, in the same proportions of foreign currencies and sterling indicated by our predecessors. We understand that this sum will not be as readily available as the other sum and we therefore give you forty-eight hours from the opening of your London bank tomorrow. We shall call again in twenty-four hours for a progress report and to give you further instructions. Do you understand?'

'Yes.'

'Then that is all.'

'No it isn't by God,' Gannon's voice snapped into the room. Even reproduced over the tape recorder it startled me. I looked at the man himself who was staring intently at the slowly revolving reels on the deck of the machine as his words were played back. 'Listen and don't interrupt and don't hang up or all deals are off.' There was a short but effective pause and then Gannon's voice continued clearly and concisely. 'First, before we agree to any deal we want assurances that the girls are alive and well. Both of them.' I looked at Tommy, like Gannon he was intent on the tape-recorder. 'We want to talk to them. Until we are sure they are well we will not begin to raise the money. Understood?' He didn't wait for a reply, but went on with the assurance of a man in complete control of events.

'I give you my word that no attempts are being made or will be made to trace this or any subsequent telephone calls, but, if you choose not to believe me, you can make further short calls. But,' his voice hardened, 'however it is done, we talk to the girls. Do you understand me?'

There was a longish pause and then the other man's voice came on, a little muffled this time. 'I'll call back.' The telephone went dead and Parker leaned over and switched off the recorder.

I looked at Gannon. 'Have they made the second call?'

'Not yet.'

'Did you . . . ?' I didn't get a chance to say anything more because, right on cue, the telephone rang and Parker flicked the switches on the recorder and Gannon picked up the receiver.

The call took a long time and both Gannon and Tommy talked to their daughters. Then the tape recorder was rewound and we all heard both sides of the conversations.

The same man started. 'Gannon? Here is your daughter. Be careful what you say. We will prevent her speaking immediately anything is said that might endanger us.'

There was a short pause and then a child's voice, not immediately identifiable as Jacintha's. Not surprisingly she sounded as if she had been doing a lot of crying. 'Daddy. Please do what they say. I'm afraid.'

Then Gannon. 'Have they hurt you?'

'No, not really. I banged my head on the roof, but that wasn't their fault.'

Gannon again. 'Listen to me now, I want proof that you are Jacintha.'

'But Daddy . . . '

'Don't interrupt.' The voice was cold and I looked at the man as he listened to his own voice. There was no expression there, none that I could read anyway. I knew and so did everyone else in the room, that he was merely doing what I had asked. Giving the girl a chance to try and tell us something. It just seemed that he might have tried to reassure her with a little warmth. It brought back to my mind the fact that when he had first been told about the kidnapping he had gone back into a meeting.

He was going on. 'Tell me something that nobody else could know.'

There was a pause and during it there were faint sounds that could have been a small girl trying not to cry. I looked at Celia Gannon. Her eyes were on her husband and the expression in them wasn't pleasant.

Then Jackie's voice came on again. She spoke for a little while, but there was nothing there that seemed to be of any use to us. It certainly confirmed that it was her, but that hadn't been the object of the exercise.

When Jenny came on there were no signs of the emotion Jackie had shown, but I knew her voice well enough to know that she wasn't as calm as she wanted her father to think.

Tommy started much as Gannon had done and then let Jenny talk. As with Jackie there was nothing that gave me any clues to where they were being held and Tommy must have sensed that because he had asked a question. 'Have you a message for your Uncle Harry? One that will help him to be sure it really is you and that you're well.' There was a slight stress to the words, 'Help him'.

Then Jenny's voice. 'Tell him I hope to

have a Sinistral Dog Whelk for my collection soon.'

That was all. The man's voice came on at that point.

'That's enough,' he said. 'Do we have a deal?' There were a few seconds of confusion as Tommy transferred the telephone to Gannon and he confirmed that he would raise the money. Then he insisted on talking to the girls again when the next call was made and that was that.

The tape recorder was switched off and we sat in silence.

Gannon broke it. 'Well? Did you get anything out of that?'

He was talking to me. 'I'm not sure,' I said. 'From Jackie we got one thing.'

'What?'

'The bit about hitting her head on the roof.'

'Yes,' Parker said. 'What do you think?'

'Might be nothing,' I said. 'Perhaps she was being carried and banged her head on a low ceiling.'

'Then she would have said ceiling, not roof.'

'Maybe,' I said. It wasn't something

171

that seemed to be of much use to us, at least not at that stage. Maybe later, if we got some indication of the location where the girls were being held.

'What in God's name was all that about a sinister dog?' Gannon asked.

'A Sinistral Dog Whelk,' I said.

'What is it?' I hadn't taken much notice of Jenny's sea-shell collecting, but I had heard her talk about Dog Whelks. It was one of the most common shells on the beach where I took her. She didn't bother with them they were like daisies to an orchid collector. I didn't know what a Sinistral shell was, but I knew the word from my crossword-puzzle days. It meant left-handed. I told them what little I knew and then left them all looking at one another and went out into the corridor and searched out Mrs. Jennings. I asked her to take me to Jenny's dormitory. She did and stood there as I looked around the little cubicle.

Like the room I had shared, briefly, with Lucinda Gannon it was a partitioned part of a larger room with thin panels that reached to within a couple of feet of the ceiling. There was a bed, standard single-size, a table and hard chair, a small upholstered chair, a chest of drawers and a small wardrobe. Everything clean, but a bit impersonal. A sort of junior league, soft-centred army barracks.

There were a few brightly coloured pictures pinned to a piece of perforated hardboard that hung on the wall above a radiator and there was a small bookshelf on top of the chest of drawers. On top of the wardrobe there was a suitcase, a larger brother of the one she used when she came with me for the weekend.

'What are you looking for Mr. Morgan?' Mrs. Jennings asked me.

'Nothing in particular,' I replied. 'Just looking in case inspiration strikes.'

'Well, I'll leave you to it. You can find your way back?'

'Yes, thank you.' She went out, closing the door behind her and I sat on the bed and looked round at Jenny's domain. I ran my eyes over the bookshelf. There were several books on shells. I pulled one down. 'Shell and shell collecting' by S. Peter Dance. I looked up Dog Whelk in the index and didn't find it. Then I looked up Sinistral and found three references all on two facing pages. I turned to the double page spread and there was the missing Dog Whelk. Its full name was European Dog Whelk and I read what the author had to tell me.

It confirmed what Jenny had told me, it was extremely common on British sea-shores. It also told me that a Sinistral Dog Whelk, a version of the common shell, but with a left-hand spiral instead of the usual right-hand form, was extremely rare. No more than half a dozen specimens found in two hundred years. That seemed to suggest that Jenny had been trying to tell me something. There didn't seem much chance of her adding one to her own collection.

I read on. One of the incredibly few, known specimens had been picked up on the beach at Scarborough, a few miles up the coast from the school. I got interested. A Scarborough collector in the nineteenth century, a man named William Bean, acquired one when his grand-daughter had found it on the beach by the pier.

There was a photograph of two Dog Whelk shells, one normal and one sinistral and that seemed to be the extent of the information I could get from the book. I re-read the passage and then considered what I had got. The short answer was, I didn't know what I'd got.

Then I went through the rest of the books and then I searched the room; drawers, wardrobe, the suitcase, I even opened up the bed, but there was nothing. Because it was so obvious, I almost overlooked the hardboard-mounted picture gallery. It contained the kind of thing I imagine small girls of that age always pin up on walls.

A couple of picture postcards from far-off places sent by school friends whose parents seemed to have more money to spend on holidays than I earned in a year, two or three pop singers who looked vaguely familiar even to me, a confirmed Frank Sinatra — Peggy Lee man. One of the wonders of sustained advertising I suppose. A couple of brightly coloured pictures of more pop singers, this time in groups, the members of which seemed intent on damaging the lens of the camera as they glared into it with expressions that seemed to combine advanced dyspepsia with too-tight trousers, but maybe they looked sexy to pre-teenagers. There were half a dozen coloured pictures of sea-shells, including a colour version of the one in the book. It didn't tell me anything more than the monochrome version. It was pasted to a piece of card together with two of the other shell pictures and one of the pop singers again. He seemed to be Jenny's favourite, a thin young man named Simon Black who was leering at the camera with what I imagine he thought was a soulful expression. He looked as if he'd just eaten something nasty. Jenny had printed 'Home Sweet Home' across the top of the card in red crayon, the letters arranged neatly between two ruled pencil lines.

I took the card down and studied it, turned it over, blank, and then folded it up and put it in my pocket. I stood up and glanced round, instinctively checking that I'd left the place tidy.

It didn't seem to warrant the Home Sweet Home tag Jenny had given it. Maybe that was a joke. Still, it was better than the place Stanley and I were living at the time. Sharing a caravan with someone as big as Stanley wasn't the easiest way to exist. The neatness and privacy of Jenny's little cubicle seemed very attractive.

I glanced round the room again. The book with the information about William Bean of Scarborough and the left-handed shell was still lying on the bed.

I tore out the two pages that seemed relevant, feeling slightly guilty at damaging the book. As I folded them and put them in my pocket with the card of photographs I made a mental note to buy Jenny a new copy for Christmas. Christmas. Less than a month away.

Unless something happened soon there was a good chance it wasn't going to be a very happy one for a lot of people.

I went down to the office. Everyone looked curious and then vaguely resentful when it was clear that I didn't intend telling them what I had found in Jenny's room.

Parker volunteered the information that his visit to the farmer and his wife had produced nothing of apparent value except that the old man had done odd jobs for the school and, for that matter, for almost everyone else in the district.

'Did you search the old man's place thoroughly?' he asked me.

'Yes.'

He grunted, the sound making it clear his confidence in my ability wasn't too strong. 'I think I'll take a look myself,' he said.

I shrugged my shoulders. If he still wanted to have something to do that seemed as good a way as any for him to spend his time. Not that I expected him to find anything.

I collected Stanley and we went out to the Volvo and with him at the wheel we headed for Scarborough. I hadn't been consciously awkward in keeping from them the information I'd uncovered about the left-handed shell. Partly it was because I didn't understand what Jenny's

178

message had meant, if indeed it had meant anything. It occurred to me, as we approached the outskirts of Scarborough, that there might have been another reason. I wasn't sure if I trusted everyone.

I played with the thought and got nowhere. There was no-one I mistrusted, nothing that I could recall that had been said or done that supported my feeling, but it was there, floating around the edges of my mind.

The first thing I found when I started trying to follow up the information I had found in the book on sea-shells was that the pier near where William Bean's grand-daughter had found one of the extremely rare sinistral dog whelk shells was no longer there. And hadn't been for a long, long time.

That crossed one possibility off my list almost before I'd started. I had to assume that Jenny knew the passage in the book well so I started on all the Beans in the telephone directory. There were twelve of them and only two had a W among their initials. I tried those two first, but I recognised that if Jenny had been trying to tell me to chase someone named Bean, it wasn't likely that she would have been too bothered about matching initials with a nineteenth century shell-collector.

Four hours later I had nothing. Ten of the twelve Beans had been home and all were clear as far as I could see. Not that I expected the people I was looking for would come to the door with a machine-gun in their hands to indicate that they were on the side of the ungodly. But I knew what the man and the woman looked like and I knew they knew me and Stanley. There would be a reaction of some kind.

In the car, outside the last of the Beans who was at home, I leaned back in the seat and rubbed my hand over my eyes. Then I reached down and massaged my ankle.

'Any more Harry?' Stanley asked. I had told him what I was doing and why.

I shook my head. 'No. That was the last.' The chances of the remaining two being the ones I was looking for seemed remote, and in any event there were probably four or five times as many Beans in the town who were not on the telephone.

'What do we do now?' A good question. I reached into my pocket and pulled the torn pages and the sheet of paper with the pasted-on pictures from my pocket. I studied the pictures of shells, re-read the passage about William Bean and came up blank. That left the picture of the pop singer, Simon Black. That didn't help either.

'Let's go back,' I said.

We were on the north side of the town and Stanley drove straight through the centre, the traffic-free, wet Sunday contrasting with what it would be like six months ahead.

We had almost cleared the town centre when I saw it. A roadside hoarding advertising a pop concert at the Futurist Theatre.

A pop concert featuring Simon Black.

15

The concert was scheduled to start at eight o'clock that night and when we parked the car on the sea-front it was still three and a half hours to curtain up, or whatever they do to start one of those things. It was dull and cloudy and would soon be dark. There were a couple of lights on in the foyer of the Futurist and I pushed open one of the swing doors and went in with Stanley close behind me.

There were a few people about, obviously staff of the theatre, and apart from a few interested glances at Stanley, none of them took much notice of us. The Futurist is part of a leisure complex that includes an extensive first floor bar, with what turned out to be an excellent view over the bay, a restaurant and one or two other bits and pieces including some typical seaside amusement halls at street level.

If Jenny had been trying to tell me they

were there then it seemed a not unreasonable assumption they would be hidden well away from the public areas. That still left a lot of ground to cover. For a start the amusement arcades were not open during the Winter, then there were the offices and the store-rooms and the backstage part of the theatre. That was where I started.

I had exhausted the possibilities of the backstage area and had decided to try the deserted amusement arcades when a small, harrassed-looking individual in a shiny dinner suit appeared and demanded to know what the hell I was doing.

I told him we were not very happy with the security for our star and he seemed to take it that I had something to do with Simon Black's encourage. He got a bit panicky and I said that as long as I could check everywhere in the time left before the performance and without further interruption, I was sure everything would be all right. He assured me I wouldn't be interrupted, turned round, saw Stanley for the first time, stepped back in alarm and then hastily disappeared to do whatever he still had to do. He looked even more harrassed and worried from the back.

The amusement arcade looked dirty and oppressive in the dim ceiling lights that came on when I tried the first bank of switches as I went through the door that led from the theatre basement into the arcade. The machines on which next year's holidaymakers would be trying to win back the many tons of pennies lost by this year's holidaymakers, looked shabby without their flashing lights. The silence was wrong as well. There should have been the clatter of machines and the clamour of people.

I had checked some of the few doors that opened off the arcade with no success and was approaching the remaining door that was at the far end of the building when I heard something. I stopped dead and listened. The noise, whatever it was, had come from behind the door I was approaching.

'Harry . . . ' Stanley started to speak, but I cut him off with a gesture. I tried to decide what I'd heard and then the sound came again and this time I was sure. It was the sound of someone crying. It could have been a man, woman or a child, but I hadn't any doubt that it was a little girl.

I was still standing there, indecisive, thinking about people being shot in the back, when the lights went out.

I had started to turn when I felt Stanley's hand sieze my arm and I felt myself lifted off my feet and then, a split-second before I crashed into an adjacent pin-ball machine with a jar that very nearly loosened my teeth, there were three shots.

The subconscious part of my brain was working before the rest of it had finished reassuring me that I hadn't been hit. I had been speaking the truth when I told Gannon that I didn't like guns, particularly when they were being fired at me but my ear was sharp enough to work out that the three shots were too close together to have come from one gun.

Two guns, maybe two people with one gun each, or one person with two guns. Either way we stood a good chance of being on the losing side. I stayed where I was and whispered to Stanley in the echoing silence. 'Where are you?'

That wasn't a very good idea and another shot crashed out and the bullet went bouncing crazily round the arcade smashing into various metallic surfaces. Then, from somewhere over our heads came a rumbling sound that gradually settled to a steady drumming. Someone had switched a generator on in the theatre above. No doubt their regular mains supply wouldn't withstand the battery of electric guitars that were due to be plugged in later on.

'Here Harry.' Stanley's voice was so close to my ear that I jumped. The movement made me aware that I had added a bruised arm to my damaged ankle. The noise of the generator made it easier to converse.

'They must be near the door we came in by,' I whispered.

'Yes Harry.'

'Take your shoes off,' I hissed and reached down and pulled off my own. In the darkness I felt around until I touched

Stanley's hands and took his shoes from him. I put all the shoes on the floor close to my right hand and then took his hand again and pointed his finger towards the wall on his left. 'Go that way,' I whispered. 'When you reach the wall, feel your way along until you come to a machine, take cover behind it or under it and then stay there. Whatever happens stay there. Okay?'

'Okay Harry.' I waited until he had gone, checking his movement away from me by touch. Then I gathered up three of the shoes under my left arm, hurled the fourth one well down the building in the direction from which the shots had come and then ran softly, bent low, towards the opposite wall to the one Stanley had gone to.

My shoe-throwing produced one shot from one of the guns. The flash told me that it was along the same wall as Stanley. Not good. I reached the false security of a machine and pulled myself up until I was standing against the wall beside it. My damaged arm banged against something and I clenched my teeth to stop a yell of pain. I carefully explored the object I had struck. It was an electrical switchbox.

I thought about it and then decided that anything was better than hovering about in the darkness waiting for someone to put the lights on when they chose to and pick us off at their leisure. I threw a second shoe to keep the opposition busy and that time I drew two shots from different places.

There were definitely two of them.

I stood the remaining shoes on top of the machine and felt along its surface and sides and its front. As far as I could tell it was one of those things that are designed to appeal to the warlike instincts of amusement arcade visitors. They have a screen on which targets appear, sometimes aircraft, sometimes tanks, sometimes warships. At the front, a simulated gun-stock and trigger. The object of the game is to destroy as many of the targets as possible. I felt around for the coin slot and tried to measure its size with my finger nail. It didn't feel big enough to take a ten penny piece and as I didn't think amusement arcade owners were in the business of being benevolent I assumed it wouldn't be for either a penny or a two penny piece. I felt in my pocket and carefully brought out the coins there, one at a time, until I located a five penny piece. I placed it in the slot, then with one hand still on the coin, I reached out and gripped the handle on the side of the electrical switch.

Before I had a chance to pull the switch there were three more shots, evenly spaced and all coming from near the door by which we had entered. I waited and then heard a faint scraping sound from close behind me. I felt my skin crawl in anticipation of a shot, but there wasn't one. Instead there was a metallic scraping sound and then a clang. It didn't take a genius to work out that the three shots had been cover for one of the opposition to reach the door I had been about to open. It had been successful and whoever it was they were now safely in the room with the little girl I had heard crying.

But that still left the one near the main entrance.

I took a deep breath and prayed that

the switch really was connected to that particular machine. I pulled the switch and the machine lit up. With the other hand I banged in the coin and then reached for the plastic trigger and squeezed.

It was like World War Two all over again. Then before anyone had time to know just what was happening I banged the main switch off again and the patch of light around me faded and I hurled myself away from that part of the arcade and lay silent listening to my heart beating and the breath scraping in and out of my lungs. Above the sounds from inside my own body I heard the door we had come in by bang shut, then footsteps fading rapidly along the passage that led to the theatre.

I took another deep breath and ran for the door. I found the light switch and pressed it down. Nobody took a shot at me. I looked round and saw Stanley, rising to his feet, smiling cautiously to show he was unharmed.

I ran back to the other end of the arcade and opened the door there. The room had a low vaulted roof and it was filled with bits of amusement machines that had succumbed to the battering their users had given them. I couldn't find the light switch but there was enough illumination coming in from the arcade to let me see that someone had been held there.

There was some sacking on the floor and, just like the cabin in the forest, there were the remains of food. I stepped cautiously into the room and eventually found a switch for the light. In the far wall there was another door and when I opened it I was in an alleyway that ran along the back of the theatre. I wasted a few minutes by checking both ways along the alley, but I didn't expect to find anyone hanging around, waiting for me. Nobody was.

I realised that I was still without my shoes and I went back into the storeroom and through the arcade, collecting my shoes and Stanley and his shoes on the way.

We went through into the theatre and the first person I saw was the man in the shiny evening suit.

'Were they with you?' he asked indignantly.

'Who?' I asked.

'Those two. That man and woman.'

'What man and woman?'

'They followed you down, then he came out alone. He knocked me down when I tried to ask him who he was.'

'Nothing to do with me,' I said. 'Where did he go?'

'Right out of the main door. Ran off along the front.'

'Did he?'

'Yes. Well . . . .' He paused and looked at me. 'Have you finished?'

I thought about that for a moment. I couldn't see much point in persisting with the search. I was certain the girls had been in the building, but all I'd succeeded in doing was to frighten the kidnappers away into another hiding place.

'Yes, I've finished,' I told the man.

'Good,' he said and went off looking as anxious and as harrassed as ever. Maybe being a private enquiry agent has its advantages after all. Being shot at by homicidal kidnappers is probably a lot less damaging to the nerves than keeping a few thousand female teenagers under control while their idols perform their musical sex act on-stage.

From the car I checked all around. There were a few more people about than there had been when we'd arrived. Not many more, and mostly youngsters arriving early for the concert. The sight of all the youngsters reminded me that the classmates of Jenny and Jackie would, by then, have returned to the school.

'Back to the school Stanley,' I said. I sat and thought about things as we went along the road.

Proximity to death has its advantages. My brain was functioning a bit better and long before we got back to the school I actually had a constructive idea.

16

The school looked more alive when we got back. Not that there were many more people in sight but there were a few extra cars in the courtyard and lights were on everywhere.

I was pleased to see that while Stanley and I had been dodging bullets in the amusement arcade everyone else had been busy in other ways. At least Tommy had.

He had talked to most of the classmates of the missing girls. He had done it alone because Mrs. Jennings had been involved in a crisis of some kind with one of the newly returned pupils. I was in time to hear the last of the conversations and when the little girl had gone off to join her friends, most of whom seemed to be clutching an apparently obligatory teddy-bear, I asked him what he had got out of it.

'Only one positive thing. Everybody

knew Simpson would be late and you would be taking Jacintha to the beach with you and Jenny.'

I nodded my head. I'd expected that, but I couldn't see if it helped.

I left Tommy and went to look for Parker and told him what had happened in the amusement arcade.

He listened to me, impassive as ever.

'Did you find anything at the cottage?' I asked.

He shook his head and changed the subject. 'Do you want to borrow a gun?'

'No. Thanks, but that's not my style.'

'What is your style Morgan?'

'Ask questions, stumble around in the dark until I trip over something.'

'Or it trips over you?'

'An alternative arrangement that occasionally occurs.'

He shook his head slowly. 'I can't make up my mind about you,' he said.

I inclined my head. 'Good,' I said. 'That makes it mutual.'

He opened his mouth to answer and then thought better of it. Mrs. Jennings came by looking a little ragged around the edges. It seemed that the last few days before the Christmas holidays were going to be fraught with plenty of problems for her as well.

'There are a couple of things I'd like you to do with all that electronic hardware you have kicking around' I said to Parker after she had passed us.

'What are they?'

'You're tape recording the incoming calls from the kidnappers?'

'Yes.'

'First I want the recorder setting up so that everything is recorded as it comes in, not just the kidnappers.'

'No problem.'

'I also want to hear the existing recordings again. If you're setting up the recorder permanently that means I'll need another machine.'

'The school will have one, several probably.'

'Okay, you get me the tapes, I'll find a recorder for myself and replay them.'

'What do you expect to hear that you didn't hear the first time?'

'I'm not **expecting** anything. There

might be something there that could help, but which we missed the first time round.'

'Okay. Anything else?'

'Not for the moment.'

'Right.' He started to turn away and then stopped and looked back at me. 'Your background doesn't suggest you're the right kind of man for this kind of job.'

'What does it suggest?'

'Waiting and watching in dark doorways for erring husbands.'

'Or wanton wives?'

He looked at me with his dark, deep-set eyes and there was the faintest glimmer of emotion in them.

'Or wanton wives,' he agreed after a moment. I seemed to have struck a nerve.

'All of which suggests that you've been checking up on me,' I said, moving on to more predictable ground.

'Of course.'

'Of course?'

'Mr. Gannon ordered it.'

'He would.'

'If your roles were reversed, wouldn't you?'

'Quite honestly I don't know what I'd

do if our roles were reversed. Some things are beyond imagining and being a multi-millionaire is one of them. Still, I take your point. He wanted to be certain that I wasn't involved in the kidnapping.'

'Yes.'

'Sometime you'll have to tell me what gems you unearthed about my past.'

'Yes,' he said. 'Sometime I will.'

'And in the meantime you're still not sure that I can cope with all this?'

'I shouldn't be, but I have to believe the evidence of my own eyes above that taken from official records.'

'So where does that leave us?'

'It leaves me trusting you,' he said. I thought I detected a note of reluctance in his voice.

'One white man who doesn't speak with forked tongue,' I said.

He didn't smile at my weak attempt at humour. 'Maybe you don't at that,' he said.

He brought the tapes and I went in search of a tape recorder. I found several of them. School isn't like it was in my days. Chalk and a blackboard was the full extent of teaching aids at my school.

The tapes didn't tell me much. The main thing I was listening for was background noise on the tapes of the two calls made by the second gang. I've seen those movies where a train whistle is heard during a telephone call and some bright spark identifies it as the five-fifteen from St. Pancras as it passes the end of Peckwater Street in Kentish Town. I doubted if it would be as easy as that, always assuming there was any background noise to hear.

On the first of the two calls the sound quality was ordinary, nothing special about it at all. On the second call, where the girls talked to their fathers, there was a hollow quality to the sound, a slight suggestion of an echo. And there was a background noise. A low rumbling sound that could have been almost anything, but which I was pretty certain was the generator in the theatre.

That was all.

I rewound the last tape, then dropped them all into my pockets, switched off the electronic teacher-substitute and left the room feeling more inadequate than usual.

Next door was the staff room, a comfortably worn place that looked like staff rooms are supposed to look; faintly bookish and well and truly isolated from the day to day turmoil of the rest of the school.

Celia Gannon and her step-daughter were there. So were two members of the staff; one, an elderly man who looked as if he was covered in a fine layer of chalk dust; the other, a youngish, athletic-looking woman who seemed slightly out of place in that rather academic place. She looked as if she would have been happier on a horse or skiing down a mountain.

I smiled at them and got a weary but pleasant smile in return from the older of the two women. Lucy treated me to a frosty glare that didn't do anything to improve her already sulky expression.

I said a few meaningless pleasantries to them, mainly aimed at keeping Celia Gannon from getting too depressed about it all. I didn't seem to have much success.

While I was doing that the two teachers

wandered out and after a while there was an awkward silence when I ran out of things to say. The silence was broken when the door opened and Mrs. Jennings appeared in the opening. 'Oh, I'm sorry. I'm looking for Mr. Benson.'

'The old boy covered in chalk dust?' I asked.

'Chalk . . . oh, yes, he does look a bit like that. Yes, have you seen him?'

'He went out a few minutes ago; he was with the netball queen.'

Mrs. Jennings glowered at me. 'Ah, Miss Potter. Yes, thank you. I think I know where they will be.' The door closed and I turned away to see Lucy looking at me with something approaching a smile on her face.

'At least you're not letting all this get you down,' she said.

'No point is there,' I said. She gave me one of her calculated looks and Celia Gannon intercepted it. She stood up and excused herself and went out. I suppose she thought she was doing the right thing, but I was sorry to see her go. Although she might not know it, she was much more my kind of woman than her step-daughter, but despite her apparent lack of rapport with her husband, she didn't seem to have a roving eye. Or at least, I corrected myself as the door closed behind her, if it roved it didn't rove in my direction.

'Well?' Lucy asked.

'Well what?'

'What now?' The conversation wasn't exactly sparkling.

'Tell me something,' I said. 'Why does your father employ bodyguards when he has a perfectly good security force?'

'Is that what you really want to talk about?'

I waved my hand round the room. 'What else can we talk about here?'

She shrugged her shoulders. 'I suppose you're right.'

'Well, why?'

'He's afraid of them.'

'Who?'

'Jay Parker and his men?'

'Afraid of them?'

'Yes.'

'Why for God's sake?'

'Can't you guess?'

I could, in fact I had, but the look in her eyes seemed to confirm it.

'I don't think I'll ever understand millionaires,' I said.

'Anything else while we're being friendly?'

'No.'

'Oh.' She sounded disappointed.

'Sorry,' I said even though I wasn't.

'I may not offer a second time,' she said.

'Oh.' I said, trying to sound disappointed. It didn't sound very convincing in my ears, but I hoped for the best. Not that I owed her anything, but she wasn't to know that casual sexual relationships are not my style. Well, almost always they're not my style. Like anyone else I get tempted on odd occasions, but I try and resist the temptation. Not for any moral reason but because there have been times when my relationships with women have caused problems with Stanley.

More often than not he has seen my affairs as a threat to the way we live, a threat to him. For that reason I do one of

two things. One is to keep my relationships with women secret from him. That
inevitably results in a furtiveness that
soon spoils things. It is also open to
discovery as happened once or twice in
the past. Even now I don't like to think
about what happened when he did find
out about them. A violent tantrum from a
small boy is bad enough, the same kind of
thing from a man of his size and strength
is something else entirely.

The other way out of the problem is to
do what I was doing with Lucy Gannon.
Avoid letting anything develop. Anyway, I
didn't fancy her all that much. Well, not
too much.

'I'm going to get some sleep,' she said,
being too obvious again. 'What about
you?' She must have forgotten she'd said
she might not offer again.

I shook my head. 'Not now. Later
maybe.'

'The offer might not be made later,' she
said.

'My loss,' I said.

'Yes.'

I stood up and went to the door. I

opened it and hesitated. 'How often did you call Jackie?' I asked.

'Here at the school?'

'Yes.'

'Hardly ever. Why?'

'No reason,' I said. I closed the door and went in search of Celia Gannon to ask her the same question and one or two others that suddenly seemed relevant.

17

I asked Celia Gannon the question I had asked her step-daughter. She usually called Jacintha once a week when she was in England although she had missed that week as she had been in France with her husband. That accounted for the fact that the slight variation in routine that Simpson had instigated hadn't been relayed back to the family.

When I went out, alone, to try and check on something else that was worrying me, I tried to be optimistic about things. I wasn't very successful, I never could fool anyone for long, certainly not myself.

I drove into Scarborough and parked on the front. There were lights on in the theatre entrance and the people I'd seen there on the previous occasion were still there. It looked as if nothing had happened until I got inside the auditorium. There it looked as if it had been used as a rescue shelter for victims of a major disaster.

The man with the shiny dinner-suit looked even more worried than before.

'What are you doing back here?' he demanded as soon as he saw me. 'You said you were with that . . . that . . . '

'Gave you some trouble did he?'

'Trouble? Bloody little big-head. Think they're God some of these singers. Singers? That's a laugh for a start.'

He seemed to have forgotten I had lied to him earlier.

'That man and woman, those who knocked you over. Remember?'

'Yes. What about them?'

'Can you describe them?'

'Describe them? Of course I can, but why should I?'

I leaned forward towards him and lowered my voice to a confidential whisper. 'Up to no good when I disturbed them. I chased 'em for a few miles, but lost 'em. Need a description to circulate to all regions.'

'Yes of course,' he whispered back. He described the man and the woman. Then

I asked him another question before I left him there in the middle of his chaos.

Five minutes later I was back on the main road, leaving the town behind me and keeping just within the speed limit. Being stopped by a policeman was something I didn't want at that moment. Particularly until I'd had time to assimilate the information from the man at the theatre.

His description of the couple had been good enough to confirm that they were the two I had seen on the beach. He had seen the woman more clearly than I had and his description rang a vague bell that wasn't clear enough to register anything positive in my mind.

The answer to the question I had asked him was more perplexing. Although he didn't often go down into the amusement arcade during the off-season he had been down there a couple of times recently and on both occasions he had been into the small workroom where I suspected the girls had been held. Quite clearly he hadn't seen anything suspicious which suggested that the hiding place had been temporary.

He had also volunteered information that was quite unexpected, but provided a stronger motive than we'd had so far for one of the murders. The man who used the workshop to repair machines was the ubiquitous Fred Rowlands. The district was going to miss him.

I began to wonder if Jenny's message really had been about the arcade. Maybe she had been trying to tell me something else and the fact that Simon Black, whose picture was in her bedroom, was appearing at the theatre was nothing more than a wild coincidence.

I conjured up a mental image of the pictures of seashells and the pages from the book I'd found in Jenny's room. They still didn't mean anything to me. That reminded me about Fred Rowland's sack of seashells. They were still in the car behind the back seat.

I stopped and spent a few minutes rummaging in the sack but I soon gave up. The only distinctive thing about them appeared to be the smell.

As I pulled up at the school, Parker was

waiting for me on the steps. I had expected he would be on the look-out for me.

'Anything?' he asked.

'Nothing I can nail to the floor.'

'I expected as much,' he said morosely as I left him.

When I reached the kitchen I could hear voices, voices I recognised. Tommy and Lucy Gannon were there.

Tommy looked up as I walked in. 'Hello Harry. Any developments?'

'Maybe,' I said. 'Where's Stanley?'

'Looking for Mister Mackay.'

'Again? It's time you had that thing converted into a pyjama case. Where did he go?'

'I didn't see.'

'Okay, I'll look for him.'

I went back down the hallway and then through most of the building looking for Stanley and the dog. There were no answering calls or barks despite all my shouting. After I'd received a few angry glares from faces peering round various doors I gave up and came to the conclusion that Mister Mackay must have demanded to be let out into the grounds.

I went out of the front door and began tramping around outside looking for the pair of them.

18

Outside a fine, slanting drizzle soaked me within seconds of going out into the grounds. Low overcast clouds were producing the rain and blanking off any stars or moonlight that might have made it easier to see.

I had fallen into the shrubbery at least twice before I decided that it would be better if I stood still and shouted for Stanley. I did. Then I shouted for the dog and that didn't have any effect either.

I gave up the idea of standing still and started off around the outer wall of the main building. I passed the window of the Principal's office and moved towards it out of nothing more than idle curiosity. A figure materialised in front of me. It was one of Gannon's bodyguards. He didn't have a raincoat over his dark grey suit, made even darker through being sodden with water.

'I'm looking for my cousin, Stanley, the big man,' I said.

'You won't find him in there,' he said quietly, jerking a thumb over his shoulder at the lighted window.

'Have you seen him?'

'No.'

'What about the dog?'

'Dog?'

'A Scottish terrier. Small, black, bites.' I felt unjustifiably irritated by the man.

'Not here,' he said. I shrugged and turned away. Around the back of the building I found myself wading knee-deep in something that could have been cabbages.

I stumbled out of that patch and found a gravelled path. I crunched my way wetly along it as it skirted the school. It came to an end beside a low door set into the wall. I stopped there and hesitated about continuing on through the long grass beyond.

Then I heard a faint yelping. I started off towards the sound and as I turned the corner I saw Stanley coming towards me. He had the dog under his arm.

'Hello Harry,' his teeth gleamed for an instant. 'I found Mister Mackay. Jenny will be pleased.'

'Yes,' I said. 'She will, when we find her.' I looked at him. He was soaked. 'How long have you been out here?'

'Some time, I'm not too sure. I couldn't find him at first. Then I did and then he got away again. He bit me as well.'

'I'm not surprised,' I said. 'That animal is friendless.' I turned away. 'Come on let's get out of this rain.'

I led the way back around the building, I didn't see Gannon's bodyguard as we passed the office window, but I didn't doubt that he was there. Once inside the building I led Stanley down to the kitchen and closed the door so that he could put the dog down.

'Take off your coat,' I told him and did the same myself. Then I put the kettle on and while it was boiling I emptied a tea-pot that stood on the drainer and searched the cupboards for tea and sugar. Milk was easy, it was in the 'fridge. There were a lot of eggs in there too.

I took out half a dozen and broke them into a bowl and started making an omelette for Stanley. While it was cooking I rinsed out the cups Tommy and Lucy had been using and poured out tea for us both.

'How do you feel?' I asked him.

'All right.' He didn't look all right, but I didn't press the point.

I emptied the omelette out of the pan onto a plate and put it in front of him. For someone who usually eats in a day more than I eat in a week he managed to view it without much enthusiasm.

'Don't worry about Jenny,' I told him. 'It won't be long now.'

'Are you sure?'

'Yes.' I wondered if I sounded as doubtful as I felt.

'It is the man and the woman who were on the beach that have taken Jenny and Jackie, isn't it?' he said, surprising me yet again.

'Looks like it.'

'Who are they Harry?'

'I don't know.'

He was silent for a few moments and

then he began to eat. After a while he stopped chewing and looked at me with a frown of concentration on his forehead. 'The lady on the beach was like Mrs. Jennings, wasn't she?' he said.

I stared at him in silence while my mind slipped a gear before catching up again. I had known that something in the theatre manager's description had been vaguely reminiscent of someone else, but I hadn't caught on. Stanley had.

After a few more moments I trusted myself to speak. 'Yes, she did look a little like Mrs. Jennings,' I said.

He went on eating. Although he had seen a resemblance he had made no further connections in his mind and in that we were about equal. I couldn't make a connection either. I shook my head as I looked at him, it seemed he hadn't lost his new-found capacity to surprise me.

He looked paler than usual. The bandage around his head was dirty and some fresh blood had seeped through it.

'Has that started bleeding again?' I asked. But before he could answer the door opened and Parker came in.

'There's been a development.' I said.

'What?' He looked surprised.

I told him about the woman and what Stanley had spotted.

'I'll make some enquiries,' he said.

'We're getting close,' I said. 'I'm sure of it. We'll have your daughter back soon.'

There was a long silence and when he spoke his voice was almost inaudible. 'What did you say?'

'Jacintha is your daughter isn't she?' He didn't answer, but another voice did. Celia Gannon had come into the room and was standing by the door.

'Yes,' she said, 'Jay is my daughter's father.'

'I thought so.'

'Was it that obvious?'

'Not all that obvious, but obvious enough to make me wonder how you have managed to fool Gannon for twelve years.'

'Maybe that's because . . . ' She broke off as the dog, seeing a gap between her legs and the open door, made a dash for freedom again.

'Oh, hell,' I said.

'I'll get him Harry,' Stanley said. 'He'll be going back to where I found him. I'll be careful not to bang my head on the low roof again this time.'

He had reached the door before it all registered. 'What low roof?' I asked.

'The basement, where the boilers are.'

'That's where the dog was?'

'Yes.'

'How did he get in there?'

'I think he got in through one of the little windows down near the ground. A few of them are broken.'

'How did you get in?'

'There's a door, near to where we were when you came.' I remembered the low door where the gravel path came to an end.

'Was it locked?' By now Parker and Celia Gannon were watching and listening intently.

'Yes it was,' Stanley said, a little reluctantly.

'Then how did you get in?'

He lowered his head. 'I'm sorry Harry, I didn't mean to damage it, but I couldn't lose Mister Mackay as well as Jenny.'

'Don't worry,' I said. 'You forced the door open?'

'Yes.'

'It was locked?'

'Not really. It was bolted.'

'From the inside?'

'Yes.'

I looked at Parker. 'That means either there's another way in or whoever bolted it was inside there all the time. Either way we'd better look. And we'd better do it carefully.'

'I'll check if there's another way in,' Parker said.

'Right, I'll go in from the outside,' I thought for a moment. 'Stanley, you come with me, if that door has been fastened up again I might need you.'

'All right Harry,' he said. 'Why are we going in the boiler room?'

'There's a chance,' I hesitated and looked at Celia Gannon. 'Just a chance that Jenny and Jackie might be down there.'

'Here?' Celia Gannon said. 'In the school all the time. Why?'

'I'll tell you later,' I said.

Parker went out and I followed him with Stanley following me.

In the corridor I stopped Parker. 'Try the main hall, see if there's a way in near the stage.' He looked at me enquiringly. 'The dog was sniffing and barking around there earlier,' I said. 'I didn't take any notice then.'

I left him there and went out into the drizzle again. Stanley and I followed the route I had taken alone a short time before and on the way I stopped near Gannon's window and called out, quietly, for the man I knew to be in the shadows. When he came up to me I asked him if the dog had just been past. He said it had.

'You are armed, I take it,' I said.

'Yes,' he said cautiously.

'Good, back us up. We might need you.' He glanced over his shoulder towards the window. 'The hell with Gannon,' I said. 'Back us up.' Something in my voice told him that this was the time to show initiative. He nodded and I moved on again with the bodyguard trailing along behind Stanley.

I kept off the gravel path. The grass, although it made my feet even wetter than they already were, had the virtue of allowing us to move in silence.

When we reached the door I motioned to the others to stay where they were and I eased up to it and tried the handle. It turned and I leaned against it. It didn't move. I went back to Stanley.

'You went in there?'

'Yes.'

'By forcing the bolt?'

'Yes.'

'And came out the same way?'

'Yes Harry.'

'Did you close the door behind you?'

'Yes.'

'So it should open easily.'

'Doesn't it?'

'No, it doesn't' I thought for a moment. 'Right,' I said eventually. 'Exactly where was the dog?'

'He came down the passage to me and I grabbed him.'

'You didn't reach the boiler room?'

'No.'

I made up my mind. 'Okay,' I told him.

'Break down the door again, then get out of the way and I'll go in.' I turned to the other man. 'You follow me, have your gun ready, but don't shoot indiscriminately. In fact don't shoot at all if you can help it. And certainly don't shoot if you can't see what you're shooting at. Okay?'

'Okay,' he said calmly. He seemed much less excited than I was. Maybe he was used to this kind of thing.

With Stanley leading we moved closer to the door and then, at a signal from me, he hurled himself at it. Whatever had been used as a make-shift bolt didn't provide any resistance at all. The door burst inwards with a splintering crash and Stanley disappeared from my sight. I threw myself forward after him. He had neglected to tell me that immediately behind the door was a flight of steps and I went tumbling down them, my already bruised arm and twisted ankle taking more punishment which forced a sharp yelp of pain from me. The steps went down about six feet and at the bottom I landed on Stanley. He stood up and as he did so I heard the thump as his head hit the roof. I stood up a little more cautiously. The roof was about five feet above the floor we were standing on. I couldn't see anything.

Then, behind me I heard a click and a beam of light shone down the steps. Gannon's bodyguard was coming down towards us, a gun in one hand and a torch in the other. In the backlight from the torch I could see no expression on his face, but he managed to convey the impression that while amateurs fell down stairs, professionals walked down.

When he reached the floor where we waited he let the torch beam play on the walls and then reached out and flicked on a light switch. Glass-cased bulkhead light fittings came on. I started to tell him that putting on lights which would tell everyone we were there wasn't a very smart thing to do, but then I remembered the noise Stanley and I had made and kept my mouth shut.

The basement area illuminated in the wall lights was about six feet wide, the ceiling vaulted with brick arches that sprang from piers at regular intervals. The arches made the roof even lower at the points where they crossed. The tunnel ran about twenty yards and then turned to the right. From somewhere in the distance I heard Mister Mackay's snappy bark.

'Follow me,' I said to the others. 'But keep well back and don't make any more noise than you have to.'

I moved off down the tunnel, crouching low so that I didn't hit my head and calling and whistling for the dog as loudly as I could. With luck, whoever was at the end of the passage would assume I was innocently dog-hunting and would not hear Stanley or the bodyguard.

I reached a point about two paces short of the turning before I stopped and turned and held out my hand for the torch. The bodyguard raised an eyebrow, but handed it to me without comment. I stepped cautiously around the corner, my breathing tight and my heart starting to hammer in my chest.

The passage stretched many yards ahead of me, but the lights illuminated only the first half of it, the rest was in darkness. The roof of the second section wasn't vaulted, but was supported at regular intervals by heavy timber joists that still provided a hazard and kept me in a low crouch. Still calling for the dog and whistling I moved along until I was within a few yards of the last light.

At that moment, as I paused, not knowing whether or not to continue, I heard noises ahead of me and then someone shouting. Jay Parker had found another way into the basement. At that moment there was a single shot.

I ran forward into the darkness, not risking switching on the torch at first, but then I realised that I was silhouetted against the light anyway and I was too easy to miss whether I used it or not. I switched on and the beam danced erratically ahead of me as I raced on. There was another turning and the sounds I could hear came from around it.

As I rounded the corner the scene before me was etched sharply in my mind in the few seconds before the lights went out.

Instead of a continuation of the passage

there was a wide, spacious area. Along one side, my left, were packing cases and boxes of all sizes, along the other side were four boilers with pipes running from them to join together in a bank of pipes that ran away towards one corner of the area where they turned and disappeared up through the roof.

In the far corner were stairs, wider and better lit than those we had entered by and lying on them was the still figure of a man. In the centre of the area laid on it's side, was a bench fitted up with a pipe vice. In front of the bench, scattered all over the floor, as if by the action of the bench being tipped over, were dozens of tools.

Behind the bench I caught a glimpse of two figures, one large and one small. That was when the whole scene was plunged into darkness, broken only by the light from my torch and a faint glow from the front of three of the boilers.

My thumb pressed instinctively onto the switch and the torch went out, but not before someone had taken the opportunity of trying a shot at me. I heard the bullet pass me and slam into the wall to my left.

I threw myself onto the floor and in the silence that followed as the echoes of the shot died away, I heard Stanley and the other man coming up behind me.

'Stay where you are,' I yelled. 'And get down.' There was another shot and this time there was no corresponding crack of the bullet striking the wall, instead there was a soft thud and a grunt of pain. Then there was silence.

I waited tense, then I heard Parker's voice. 'Morgan, you okay?'

'Yes, you?'

'They can't get out this way.'

'That's it then,' I said. 'You heard that, both ways out are blocked. Give up now and nobody gets hurt.'

There was a long silence, broken only by a low rumbling from the boilers.

Then a voice. I recognised it too, the voice from the same telephone call. 'Get out all of you, and remember we have the girls and they're the ones who will be hurt first.'

I had seen a small shape that could

have been one of the girls and everything now pointed to them being there, but I had to check.

'Prove you have the girls there,' I said.

There was a short silence and then Jenny's voice, unsteady and higher-pitched than usual. 'Uncle Harry, is that you? Please . . . ' Her voice was cut off abruptly and then there was a sound that could have been a struggle and then a blow and then a scream. It was the scream that did it. From behind me I heard a low murmur that changed into a roar of anger and I heard footsteps pass me, moving swiftly towards the place where the scream had come from. Stanley.

'Stanley,' I yelled and at the same time I came up to my feet and hurled myself forward, hoping to cut off his progress. Even if I'd reached him I don't suppose I would have been able to deflect him from his course. As it was I didn't reach him. Instead I hit one of the cross beams with a force that threw me onto my back. Dazed, I fumbled with the torch I still held and pressed. Somewhere in my mind was the illogical thought that the light would attract attention to me and away from Stanley and the two girls. Illogical, because self-sacrifice isn't my style.

In the light from the torch I saw that there was no need for concern about my own safety. There were too many things for the opposition to worry about without having time to shoot me. Stanley reached the bench, which must have weighed two hundred pounds, and with one hand flicked it aside as if it was nothing. Behind it were Jenny and Jackie and the man and woman I'd seen on the beach. They both had guns, but neither had time to use them as Stanley swept through them like an Arctic ice-breaker among cocktail-party ice-cubes. Unfortunately Stanley's attention was on the girls, not the people with the guns. He swept the girls up in his arms and continued his progress towards the stairs where I could see Parker moving down, a gun in his hand.

The woman recovered first and threw one shot off at Parker. I saw the man turning towards me and I flicked off the torch, dived away to my right and yelled at Stanley to get down.

I don't know how many shots were fired. At least six I would guess, but it was like a continuous barrage for just a few seconds and then there was silence. In it I heard the rumbling of the boilers. I held my breath, trying to hear any movement from anyone. Then I realised there was something different about the rumbling. It was getting louder.

I pointed the torch at the direction of the sound and pressed the switch after a short prayer to the patron saint of enquiry agents.

One of the bullets had ripped through an oil-feed pipe. As I looked at it, a flame licked out from the main jet and I swung away.

'Out,' I yelled. 'Get out, fast.' I started across the floor and in the light from my torch and the growing flame I saw the man and woman were laid on the floor. The man was alive but obviously hurt. The woman wasn't moving.

'This way.' It was Parker's voice and he reached Stanley and the girls. I didn't have time to see what had happened to

Gannon's bodyguard before there was a sudden, brighter flash of flame. I spun round, looked once at the boiler, and yelled at the top of my voice, barely making myself heard over the roar.

'It's blowing up, get down.' Then I threw myself to the floor as the boiler exploded.

It could have been a lot worse. Only just perhaps, but it could have been.

Fortunately only one boiler went up, the other three didn't. If they had, that would have been the end of everything, including, probably, the building. Even without the others it was bad enough.

The main force of the explosion went upwards and immediately above the boiler was one of the heavy timber cross beams. The beam, the breadth and thickness of a railway sleeper, splintered and the two shattered ends dropped downwards.

I scrambled to my knees and looked round, the scene clearly lit by burning oil. Parker, Stanley and the two girls were together, beyond the boiler. The man and the woman were still on the floor close to the bench. Gannon's man was standing near the entrance to the passage we had come in by, reloading his gun, one arm stiff and awkward with blood showing on his sleeve.

'You'd better get out,' he said to me, casually, pointing at the sagging roof beam. 'If that comes down, you're dead.' I looked where he was pointing and as if on cue the beam dropped a few inches and as it did so some of the brickwork in the roof fell out and clattered onto the floor in a small cloud of mortar dust.

Before any of us had time to move Stanley pushed Jenny and Jackie towards Jay Parker and leaped forward to the beam. He positioned himself beneath it and then slowly eased himself up until his back was braced against it. The trickle of dust continued pouring down, but the creaking stopped.

'Okay Stanley,' I said, my voice quiet and a lot steadier than I felt. 'Don't push it up, just stay there while the girls get out.' I gestured at Parker without taking my eyes off Stanley or the beam. I heard them move away and after what was only a few seconds, but felt like an age, I heard Parker's voice.

'Okay, we're on the stairs.' He spoke softly as if afraid that to speak loudly would dislodge more of the brickwork.

'Get right out,' I said. I looked at the man and the woman. He had fallen forward over her. I didn't know whether they were dead or merely unconscious. Certainly they would get out only if someone carried them.

As quickly as I could I dragged the man across the floor towards Gannon's body-guard. Then I crawled back for the woman.

'Okay?' I said to Stanley.

'Yes Harry, but hurry, Something is moving.' As he spoke I heard a grating sound and then more bricks fell around him and smashed onto the floor.

'Stanley, get ready to run for the stairs where the girls went. As soon as you're set run for it, don't stop and don't turn back whatever happens.'

'What are you going to do?'

'Don't worry, I'm going the other way, through the passage.'

'All right Harry, I'm ready.'

I turned and siezed the woman by the arms and dragged her across the floor, then I turned and yelled. 'Right.'

Stanley dropped to his knees and then ran for the stairs at the far corner of the room.

Nothing happened. I stayed where I was and then behind me I heard the bodyguard moving off down the passage. I looked round. He'd left the man and the woman for me. I pulled them, one at a time, down the passage to the first corner. As I reached there for the second time, I breathed deeply, glad to be out of there.

Then, unbelievably I heard a voice from the boiler room. It was Stanley's.

I ran back, still crouched low, towards the flickering light of the flames. He was in the middle of the room.

'For Christ's sake, what are you doing?' I yelled.

He looked round at me, his face concerned. 'I can't find him,' he said.

'Who?' I yelped.

'Mister Mackay.' I was unable to answer. I couldn't believe that he'd gone back in there for a dog. 'Jenny wanted him,' he added as if that explained everything. I suppose it did, to him.

'Stanley . . . ' I started to say and then I saw the dog, it had been hidden under a box, probably deeming that the safest place to be, with people shooting guns and blowing things up. Stanley saw him and reached out and at that moment there was an ear-splitting crack and then a roar as the roof gave way and everything vanished in a cloud of dust.

I scrambled across the floor and fumbled for the stairs. I pulled myself up them and then I felt a hand grip my arm and drag me the rest of the way.

'What happened?' It was Parker.

'What do you think happened, for God's sake?' I snarled at him.

I turned and looked at the billowing clouds of dust that rolled up from the boiler room. Then, out of the clouds, looking even bigger than ever, came Stanley, covered in dust and with blood streaming from the wound on his forehead, the bloodstained bandage hanging uselessly around his neck.

One huge hand was wrapped around the dog which was more white than black under its coating of dust.

I stared at Stanley and then his teeth gleamed in a wide smile that threatened to split his face open.

'Hello Harry,' he said. 'I've got the dog.'

19

It took some time to gather everyone together and begin the patching up.

Gannon's bodyguard, who had suffered only a flesh wound in the upper arm, took one of his colleagues back around the exterior of the building to bring in the man and the woman. He wasn't there. His injury must have been less serious than we'd thought. The woman hadn't been so lucky. She was dead.

Jay Parker was unhurt, but his customary calm exterior was ruffled.

Neither Jenny nor Jackie had been harmed in any way and apart from the fact that they had been frightened they were soon chattering happily; Jenny to Tommy, and Jackie to her mother.

Stanley's head wound was bleeding a lot, but he seemed oblivious to it as he wandered from group to group smiling broadly and still clutching Mister Mackay in one hand.

That left me. I was fine. If you discount the ankle that was hurting more than ever, my arm, my ribs that felt broken, and the stinging on my face where I had been singed by flames from the boiler.

Not that I had time to feel sorry for myself. Within minutes we were knee deep in small girls in nightdresses and pyjamas, milling about excitedly, wanting to know what all the noise was about.

The boiler room was located directly under the main assembly hall and there was a hole in the floor big enough to drop a bus through.

Quite a few windows had been blown out, but there were no obvious signs of structural damage. At least not to my untrained eye. Even so it was obviously going to take time and money to check things thoroughly before that part of the building could be used again, and before the boilers could be replaced.

Fortunately, the dormitories were in another part of the building and evacuation didn't seem necessary. That meant that there was somewhere for the hordes of small girls to go — back to the beds the explosion had brought them out of, but it took the staff some considerable time to shepherd them all back.

Benson, the elderly teacher, took charge of the operation with only one or two pointed cracks about the whereabouts of Mrs. Jennings.

He wasn't the only one who wanted to know where she was.

I managed a few words with him and I had begun to put the pieces together when I finally disentangled myself from the chaos and dropped wearily onto the leather settee in the Principal's office with Gannon behind the desk and looking neither pleased nor disturbed at events and with Tommy looking merely relieved.

'Has anyone seen Mrs. Jennings?' I asked.

'No,' Tommy said and Gannon shook his head.

'We'd better start looking for her.'

'She hasn't anything to do with all this has she?'

'I'm not sure whether she has a direct involvement, but she certainly has an indirect connection. The dead woman was her sister.'

'How do you know?'

'Benson, the teacher, identified her. From his description the man is her husband.'

'His name's Lennard, Arthur Lennard,' Gannon said.

I looked at him, trying to see any expression in his eyes. When it became obvious he wasn't about to enlarge on his statement I opened my mouth to ask the obvious question.

Tommy beat me to it. 'How do you know?'

'The first telephone call from the kidnappers,' Gannon said. 'We traced it to their house, it's a few miles up the road from here.'

'How long have you known that?'

'Not long. The place was empty when we searched it.'

'Apparently you didn't think it was necessary to tell me,' I put in.

'Don't be petulant Morgan,' Gannon said. 'You weren't around to be told. Anyway despite the documents we found it didn't help tell us where the girls were hidden.'

'What documents?'

'Lennard and his wife own this place.'

'The school?'

'Yes.'

'But . . . '

'That's why they wanted the money. This place is in the firing-line if the government changes its attitude towards private schools. If it is closed down they would have a building nobody would want and even if they did, it's mortgaged up to the hilt.'

'Do you think Mrs. Jennings knew about the kidnap?'

'I don't know, maybe, maybe not. I'd feel happier if I knew where she was.'

I nodded my head. 'So would I.'

'So what do we do now?' Tommy asked.

'There's not a lot we can do. We can't suddenly bring in the police. Not after concealing a kidnapping and several murders.

'Her car is missing,' Gannon put in.

I looked at him, masking my irritation. 'Is it?' I said.

'Yes.'

'Anything else you don't think I should know?'

'The Rolls was in the garage of Lennard's house.'

'Thank you' I said shortly. 'I'm glad you're taking me into your confidence at last.'

He ignored that.

'You said Lennard had been hit by a bullet,' Tommy said.

'I assumed he had been. He went over and he stopped shooting.'

'If he was hurt, he'll need attention.'

'We can't check doctors and hospitals. We haven't the manpower.'

'We . . .'

'No, we can do nothing but wait.'

'Wait for what?'

'Either Mrs. Jennings is uninvolved, in which case she'll make contact with us, or she's involved in which case the chances are we'll never see her again.'

'It isn't very satisfactory.'

'Nothing ever is,' I said, putting on my

philosopher's hat. 'I think I need a drink,' I added.

'I've looked, there's a bottle of cream sherry in Mrs. Jennings desk.'

'I'll settle for coffee.'

We went down to the kitchen. Not all of us, just Tommy and I. Gannon seemed to want to make some telephone calls. The fact that it was Sunday didn't seem to affect his business. It appeared that the sun never set on International Oil, at least not as long as there was a dollar to be made.

In the kitchen Jenny and Jackie were eating sardines on toast. I gathered the menu was by special request. Celia Gannon had prepared their repast. She had also made Stanley an omelette. I looked at my watch and tried to work out how long it had been since I'd done the same thing for him. It wasn't very long ago, but he was digging in with considerably more enthusiasm. Maybe he had more appetite now, or maybe Celia Gannon's touch with a frying pan was better than mine.

Jenny came over and put her arms

around my neck and gave me a more than generous kiss. 'Thank you Uncle Harry,' she said. 'I knew you'd come when I gave you my clue.' I looked at her blankly. I had already told myself that her message hadn't really contained a clue, that the left-handed shell and the pop singer had been quite unconnected with the fact that she had been hidden in the boiler room of the school.

'Yes, how did you work that out?' Tommy asked.

'Er,' I said. I looked at Jenny. 'You tell them.'

'They were keeping us in the boiler room, but then you made them take us to where we could talk on the telephone. They argued about going to their home, but the man said you might trace the call. So they took us to the theatres instead because they had a key for the basement door. I knew they were planning to bring us back here, that's why I said something about a Sinistral Dog Whelk shell. I knew Uncle Harry would find the picture in my room. It's on a piece of card with 'Home Sweet Home' written on it. That told him we would be at the school, and the card was hanging over the radiator and that told him to look in the boiler room. Didn't it?' The last was to me and I swallowed and nodded my head. 'I knew you'd work it out,' she said proudly.

'The bit about the pop singer helped,' I said weakly.

'Who?' she asked.

'Simon Black.'

'What did he have to do with it?'

'His picture was on the same piece of card.'

She looked blank. 'Oh, him. I'd forgotten his picture was there. I don't like him anymore.'

'Oh,' I said. There was a thoughtful silence. At least my silence was thoughtful, I can't speak for the others.

'Didn't you know he was appearing at the theatre?' her father asked.

She nodded her head. 'Yes, but he's too old. He was twenty last year,' she said, as if that explained everything. Maybe it did.

'Come on,' Tommy said. 'Let's go up and get your things packed.'

'Why?'

'You're breaking off early for Christmas,' he told her.

'Oh, good,' she said.

'Yes,' I put in. 'Mr Benson is closing the entire school tomorrow. There'll be an inspection of the building and apart from that there'll be no heating or hot water now.'

They went to the door and Tommy opened it and then looked back at me.

'See you later Sherlock,' he said. 'I'll talk to you before we go.' He glanced down at Jenny and then looked back at me. 'Don't worry,' he added, grinning. 'Your secret's safe with me.'

Neither Celia Gannon nor I spoke for a few moments.

'What was that supposed to mean?' she said eventually.

'Private joke,' I said. There was no point in telling her that I had completely misunderstood Jenny's clue and as a result had nearly got myself and Stanley shot. And there was certainly no point in telling her that I had been led to the girls by nothing more than the activity of a small dog.

Jay Parker came into the kitchen and nodded at me, unsmiling. His eyes moved on to Celia Gannon and then to Jacintha.

'Can I ask you a personal question?' I asked.

Celia Gannon looked down at her daughter. 'Go and say good-bye to Jenny,' she said. The little girl ran out and down the corridor towards the main staircase. Celia Gannon looked at me enquiringly.

'How have you managed to fool Gannon for twelve years?' I said.

'He hasn't been fooled.'

'You mean he really does know she isn't his daughter?'

'Yes, of course.'

'And does he know that you're her father?' I asked Parker. He nodded his head. I looked at Celia Gannon. 'Why does he tolerate it?'

'For reasons I can't begin to guess at. Of course Jacintha thinks he really is her father and she loves him. That makes her exceptional in my husband's world, unique in fact. Most people dislike him, quite a lot hate him. She is the only one who loves him. That makes her special to

247

him in a way I don't suppose even he fully understands.'

'But why does he keep Parker around?' I said.

'Because he is a very complex man. He probably hates Jay more than anyone else in the world, more even than he hates me. Keeping him around his daughter is a permanent punishment.'

'Why do you stay with him? What's to stop you going off together, you and Jay.'

'Because that way we would lose our daughter,' she said simply.

'You could take her with you.'

'No. For one thing my husband would take her back. The courts would almost certainly be on his side and, even if they were not, he is so powerful he makes his own rules. For another thing, Jackie would never understand why I had taken her away from her ... father.' She glanced apologetically at Parker.

I shook my head slowly. 'I thought I led a complicated life,' I said.

Celia Gannon glanced at Stanley who had finished eating and was watching us, listening carefully but, as far as I was aware, with not much understanding.

'I don't think you do,' she said. 'In fact, I think you have quite a lot to be thankful for.'

I looked at her enquiringly. 'What does that mean?'

'Your problem, if it is one, is constant. It might not help you solve it, but at least it should help you to understand it.'

'Maybe,' I said. The conversation was getting too deep and I was relieved when Tommy opened the door and looked in.

'We're on our way,' he said.

I went out into the corridor and Parker and Celia Gannon followed me. Stanley did too, after stopping to pick up the dog who was beginning to look a little irritable.

There was a clatter of feet and the two girls came down the stairs and along the corridor towards us.

'Uncle Harry, you and Stanley are coming to stay with us for Christmas,' Jenny informed me.

'Are we? Thank you Jenny.' I glanced at Tommy who nodded cheerfully.

'Unless you've got something better to do,' he said.

'No,' I said. 'We haven't got anything better to do.'

'We'll see you in a couple of weeks then.'

'Right.' I remembered something 'Jenny, there's a sackful of shells in the back of my car. Nothing special, just Dog Whelks. Take them with you if you like.'

She called out her thanks as she went down towards the main door with her father and with Stanley following on with the dog.

I turned back to Parker and Celia Gannon. 'I'll be seeing you,' I said.

'Goodbye Mr. Morgan,' Celia Gannon said and held out her hand. I took it and smiled at her. She smiled back and, although she had got her daughter back, there was still more sadness than happiness in her eyes.

She took Jackie by the hand and started off down the corridor. The little girl said to her mother. 'I want to see Daddy before we go,' and the two of them went to the door of Mrs. Jennings' office. I looked at Parker and there was more expression in his face than I'd seen before. I looked away. I've never been comfortable with other people's distress.

After a moment or two he spoke to me, his voice not quite under control. 'I underestimated you earlier,' he said.

I shrugged. 'Luck,' I said. Then I changed the subject back again because his relationship with Gannon and Gannon's wife had made me curious. 'How can you stand it?' I asked.

He didn't have to ask what I was talking about. 'What makes you think I can,' he said.

'Appearances aren't everything. There are times when I want to kill Gannon. But that wouldn't solve anything.'

'Is that why he has bodyguards who aren't part of the security set-up?'

'Yes. He knows I would like to see him dead.'

'I still don't see why he doesn't fire you and have done with it.'

'Then he would have to find somebody else to hate and humiliate.'

'I haven't noticed any humiliation.'

'Haven't you? What do you think that is?' He jerked his head savagely at the closed door of the office. Then he shrugged his shoulders. 'That's the way it is,' he said. 'I'll say good-bye Morgan.'

We shook hands. Then I asked. 'Where did you hide the bodies?'

'Where they won't be found.'

'The old man as well?'

'No, not him. He'll be found in his burnt-out van. That gets you off the hook.'

'What about the bullet in his back?'

'Don't worry about it.'

'I'm the worrying kind.'

'Trust me.'

I nodded. 'I do,' I said. I did too.

I stepped back as the office door opened and Celia Gannon came out and walked down the corridor towards the main entrance. She looked back once at Parker, but the little girl didn't.

As they went out of the door Parker turned away and went back towards the kitchen. 'I'll make some fresh coffee,' he said. 'Do you want some?'

'No,' I said. 'We still have to find Lennard and Mrs Jennings and Simpson.'

'To say nothing of some other unfinished business,' a voice said softly, close behind me. I turned round. It was Lucy Gannon.

'I thought the offer wouldn't be made again,' I said.

'Follow me up,' she said.

'Where are you going?'

'Same place as before.'

'Surely . . . '

'That was Jackie's room. Didn't you know?'

'No, I didn't, anyway that's no use. There are only thin partitions . . . '

'Then we'll have to take care we don't make any noise,' she said and started up the stairs. I stood there until she was out of sight wondering what she saw in me — not out of modesty, I'm short on that, but out of genuine curiosity. I would've thought there would be queues of eligible young men anxious to get into bed with the daughter of Carl Gannon. Maybe that was her problem.

I wasn't alone in the hall for long.

Stanley came back into the building complete with Mister Mackay, still on his lead.

'Are we going soon, Harry?' he asked.

It seemed like a good idea. 'Yes,' I said, but I couldn't help glancing up the staircase.

'I don't like her,' Stanley said.

I hadn't realised he had seen me talking to Lucinda. 'Why not?' I asked.

'She doesn't mean what she says.'

I thought about that. 'You're probably right.' I looked at the dog. 'What have you got that thing for?' I asked.

He looked guiltily at Mister Mackay. 'Jenny said I could keep him until Christmas.'

I started to say a very definite, no, but then thought better of it. 'Okay,' I said instead and a half-smile came onto his face, but he still looked guilty. 'What else is wrong?' I asked.

'I didn't know you were giving the sack of shells to Jenny.'

It was my turn to feel guilty. 'I'm sorry Stanley, I thought you had enough of that kind of shell in your collection.' That wasn't true, I hadn't thought about it at all.

'Oh, I don't mind Jenny having them, it's just that, well, I looked through the sack earlier and took some of them for myself.'

'That's all right, she won't mind.'

'She'll miss this one,' he said gloomily. He fumbled in his pocket and handed me a shell. I took it, looked at it, looked at him. 'It's left-handed,' he said.

'But the book said that only about six of these have been found in the last two hundred years.'

He nodded miserably. 'Yes.'

'And I gave them to Jenny.'

Stanley nodded again. 'Yes Harry. Shall I take it back?'

'Maybe you'd better,' I said and held it out to him. At that moment someone came in through the front door and we both looked up and Mister Mackay took the opportunity to make a break for freedom. Stanley overbalanced and knocked my hand and the shell fell to the floor. At that same moment Stanley stepped forward and tried to grab the dog's lead. He missed, but his foot crashed down on the shell.

He raced after the dog who was busily snapping at the ankles of the new arrivals.

I didn't move. I couldn't. I stood, staring down at the remains of the shell. It was crushed out of recognition, most of it down to powder.

'Well,' I said after a long moment. 'That settles that.' I glanced along the corridor. Stanley had managed to grab hold of the dog again. The new arrivals came further down the corridor.

One was Mrs. Jennings. The other was a policeman.

It took some explaining. Even when we had done, the policeman wasn't too happy about things. Mrs. Jennings played it by ear and she seemed happy enough with the outcome.

We, Gannon and I, produced an unscripted story that accounted for the fact that Mrs. Jennings had run off the road at high speed. That was where the policeman had found her, sitting in her ditched car looking shaken and pale, but apparently unhurt with her brother-in-law halfway through the windscreen and very dead.

We told him that after the boiler had burst they had panicked and instead of remaining to calmly telephone for aid as the rest of us did, they had rushed off to bring assistance.

The constable looked at her and his expression clearly said that she didn't look the type to panic, but with everyone agreeing with everyone else he decided against arguing.

Eventually he gave up trying, but I didn't look forward to what would happen when his report went in. Even his superiors wouldn't get much out of Gannon and his ability to finance a cover-up.

But what they could do to me was a very different matter. Even though Parker had done a lot of seemingly efficient covering-up there were still a few loose ends. Like Simpson the chauffeur. I hoped he was alive, not because I had any love for him, but because that way he'd take care to keep himself out of everybody's way. Particularly the police.

But if he was dead he might turn up at an awkward moment. I pushed the thought from my mind. There are some things you have to live with and it looked as if that was one of them.

After the policeman had gone I opened the office door and went back in. Mrs. Jennings told us what had really happened.

Her brother-in-law had forced her to drive him in her car. She hadn't been a willing accomplice, but his gun had effectively removed any arguments she might have had.

It seemed he hadn't been hit by a bullet. When Stanley bowled over the bench he had broken his forearm and had been badly winded. He had seen the general confusion as a means of getting away.

He had displayed enough signs of instability to convince her that he was no longer responsbile for his actions. She seemed to accept that, I suppose she had to, after all, he'd been married to her sister for over thirty years. Added to that he'd been Mrs. Jennings' employer for the last fifteen of them.

'What happens now?' I asked her. She looked blank. 'About the school,' I added.

She shook her head. 'I expect it will have to close,' she said. 'Debts, the mortgage, the repairs we now need.'

Gannon cleared his throat. 'Do you know where your brother-in-law kept the balance sheets?'

She nodded and rummaged in her desk and produced a large envelope.

He began to leaf through the papers it contained and fired occasional questions at her.

Apart from being way over my head it all sounded very dull.

I went out and closed the door behind me. Stanley was still waiting for me.

I looked up the stairs and thought about Lucy Gannon waiting for me in the little cubicle, silent, so as not to disturb all the sleeping children round her.

'I'm sorry I stood on the shell Harry,' Stanley said interrupting my thoughts.

'What?' He was looking down at the crushed remains of the Sinistrel Dog Whelk shell. The equivalent of several months, maybe a year's, earnings.

'Never mind,' I said. 'Easy come, easy go.'

We went out to the car. It was starting to get light as we drove out of the gates. Stanley was driving and I stretched my legs out in front of me and thought about the not-very comfortable bed in the caravan near York. It would seem like heaven when I dropped into it.

Thinking about bed made me think about Lucinda, still waiting for me in the school.

I came to the conclusion that, whichever way I looked at it, it hadn't been a very good weekend for me. Not very good at all.

THE END

Other titles in the
Linford Mystery Library:

DEATH SQUAD

Basil Copper

Lost in a fog on National Forest terrain, Mike Faraday, the laconic L.A. private investigator, hears shots. A dying man staggers out of the bushes. Paul Dorn, a brilliant criminal lawyer, is quite dead when Mike gets to him. So how could he be killed again in a police shoot-out in L.A. the same night? The terrifying mystery into which Faraday is plunged convinces him that a police death squad is involved. The problem is solved only in the final, lethal shoot-out.

DEAD RECKONING

George Douglas

After a large-scale post office robbery, expert peterman Edgar Mulley's fingerprints are found on a safe and he lands in jail. The money has never been recovered, and three years later Mulley makes a successful break for freedom. The North Central Regional Crime Squad lands the case when a 'grasser' gets information to them. But before Chief Superintendent Hallam and Inspector 'Jack' Spratt can interrogate the informer, he is found dead. Then, a second mysterious death occurs . . .

THE SILENT INFORMER

P. A. Foxall

A man found murdered in a quiet street brings the police a crop of unpleasant problems. But when the victim is found to have a criminal record, an affluent lifestyle, and no visible honest means of support, the problems proliferate. It seems there could be a lot of villains who wanted him dead. The Catford detectives suddenly find themselves immersed in new enquiries into apparently unrelated crimes of two years ago, which can now be seen to add up to a murderous conspiracy.